THE RANCHER'S MAIL ORDER BRIDE

Mail-Order Brides of Sweet, Texas, Book Three

ELIZABETH CHASEN

The Rancher's Mail Order Bride

Mail-Order Brides of Sweet, Texas, Book Three

Mail-Order Brides of Sweet, Texas, historically inspired clean and wholesome romance.

The biggest, tallest matchmaking cupid of the west strikes again…Big John Wiggins a widower who knows the joys of a happy marriage and the six foot, five inch widower has decided the men of his town need wives and joy too. Even if it takes him to bring the women to them.

Rancher Sam McKay has just found out he's the newest recipient of a mail-order bride, compliments of the mystery matchmaker of Sweet, Texas. But Sam has no plans to have a wife, until he realizes a marriage of convenience is exactly what he needs.

Megan Scott needs a husband, needs protection and she needs it quick. Becoming a mail-order bride to a rancher who didn't actually want a bride but is willing to marry her for a marriage of convenience will work. But that's before she realizes that she could love her new groom. But can Sam ever feel the same?

CHAPTER ONE

Sam McKay was tired of having to buy baked goods at the new bakery in town. He was grateful that three ladies in town had opened the bakery recently. Their delicious pastries and pies helped him satisfy his sweet tooth since he had no wife to bake them for him and he didn't wish to have one. At least, there hadn't been a wish before. Lately, he'd begun feeling restless and unsatisfied in many other aspects of his life. He'd begun to wish for more in his life…

More comforts in his home.

More baked goods. He'd begun to wish for the

scent of warm bread baking in the oven and fresh apple pies cooling on the counter. He'd had a dream recently of a sweet-scented woman waiting for him when he came in from the fields. She had a dusting of flour and sugar on her cheek and he'd kissed it off the moment he'd walked into the house.

Like a bandit in the night, the thought slammed into him and he tried to force it away with a determined kick.

But it had grabbed hold like a cowboy determined not to get thrown by a wild horse.

There had to be more to life than just working from sunrise to sunset. He knew there was; he'd witnessed it in others. Like the preacher and the sheriff, who'd both recently married and had a joy shining in their eyes that he envied. That contentment that was obvious now stirred this new dissatisfaction he was experiencing.

He wanted more joy in his life.

But it was a fantasy. He worked from daylight till dark and it wasn't fair to bring a woman all the way out here and leave her stranded during the day while he worked.

He and his younger brother, Gil had been working the family ranch alone for the last couple of years since losing their parents to a bad fever. He knew firsthand that life out West was hard and unforgiving.

He'd dealt with their deaths the only way he'd known how; he'd thrown himself into continuing their dream of building the ranch. It was lonesome out here. The ride into town took about four hours and he didn't go into town unless he had to because it took him away from his chores for too long. But he would have to go this week.

Standing beside the fence, he wiped sweat from his brow and stared out across the expanse of pasture to watch as Chauncey Todd, the old miner, who had a small camp at the corner of Sam's ranch, rode toward him on his mule, Tidbit.

"A mighty fine mornin' to ya, Sam," Chauncey called, then spat a stream of tobacco out and grinned widely.

Sam studied the man and his uncharacteristic good humor. "What's got you smiling this morning? Did you hit gold?"

The grizzled man grinned wider as his mule stopped in front of Sam. "Naw, jest got a message fer you from Big John Wiggins at the feed store. Since I was on my way back from town, he asked me to deliver it to you. It's about the stagecoach that's arriving tomorrow." He scratched his scraggly beard. "Looks like important business."

"Did you order something?" Gil asked. Excitement lit his face.

"No." Sam frowned. "I don't have any business with the stagecoach."

The feed store that Big John owned was the official stage stop in town. If there were messages that needed forwarding from passengers of the stagecoach, they sent them through telegraphs in care of Big John. But Sam had no business with the stage.

Chauncey spat tobacco. "I'm jest delivering the envelope with the message in it." He held it out.

"Go on, read it," Gil urged.

Sam took it and stared at the front, then turned it over and studied the back.

"Well, don't just stare at it." Gil moved closer.

He shot his little brother a glare then opened the envelope and pulled the page from inside.

Sam McKay your mail-order bride, Miss. Megan Scott, will be arriving on the stagecoach tomorrow and will need you to pick her up.

Sam scowled in disbelief at the letter, then at Chauncey. "*Who* sent this?"

"Big John. He said it was urgent. Said he found the note slipped under the door when he opened the store this morning. Said he was just passing the message on so the poor woman wasn't left standing alone in front of his store. Said it was *ur*-gent. What else does it say that makes you turn so green?"

"It says *my* mail-order bride is arriving tomorrow."

Gil's jaw dropped. "You ordered a *mail-order bride*?"

"We been wonderin' who was gonna get the next one." Chauncey's grin widened. "You going to go get her?"

Sam's eyes narrowed and he glared at his brother

and Chauncey. "I didn't order a mail-order bride. This has to be a joke."

"I bet it ain't. The sheriff and the preacher both done got themselves a mail-order bride and neither one of them ordered one either. But, they sure are happy. And I, fer one, am too. That there is one good bakery the preacher's bride opened with Ambrosia Mulberry and Essie Jane Tate. I got me a bag of goodies right thar in my saddlebag. It looks like tomorrow is gonna be your lucky day."

Gil was nodding like a tree limb caught in a tornado at Chauncey's longwinded declaration. "It's true and you know it, Sam."

Anger drew his brows together. "This is not right. Who in this town is luring these women here? I'm going to town, and if this poor woman really is on that stage, I'm sending her back home. This is cruel, tricking these women like this."

Chauncey looked puzzled. "The preacher and the sheriff's wives don't seem to think it was cruel. Seems like they're real happy. They're both smiling. And the sheriff's little daughter is all happy now that she's got her a mama. And like I said, me and you and all the men folks in town are happy about the bakery going in. So, it jest don't seem cruel at all to me."

"I agree with Chauncey. Think about it, Sam. We could get us some good meals cooked in the evenings. We wouldn't have to eat so many beans."

That was tempting. Sam took a slow breath and tried to calm his temper. He did like the bakery like Gil said but it wasn't enough to let the ridiculousness of this letter overtake his good sense. They didn't get treats often and that bakery was like heaven when they did get to town. But still that didn't change the fact that some poor female was about to find out that she didn't have a groom waiting on her.

He thought about it and another truth hit his conscience. He growled with frustration and stared down at the letter, his thoughts churning. "The one thing I can't do is have her getting off the stage thinking she's meeting me and no one be there to meet her. Not after she's already been lured out here by someone posing as me." He gritted his jaw then sighed. "So, I guess I'm going to have to go in to town and meet her. And then tell her the truth."

Chauncey crossed his arms and spat another long stream of tobacco. "I'm thinkin' tomorrow is going to be an interestin' day to be in town. I might jest load up and go back just to see you meet your new bride. You sure yer goin' to send her packin'? You seem lonely out here."

"I am sending her packing and I'm fine. You live all the way out here and you're okay."

Chauncey looked undeterred. "I'm an old geezer. But you're a right young man and you need a wife. Maybe this matchmaker in Sweet knows this. I been watchin' and it looks to me like whoever it is pretending to be you fellas and luring these pretty ladies out here ain't doing it carelessly. Seems to me, whoever it is is picking you out carefully."

Sam might have thought that about the sheriff and the preacher but why him? "I don't care what their reasoning is. I can find my own wife when I'm good and ready," he grunted.

"If that's so, then where is she?" Gil asked, defiant.

Chauncey scratched his whiskered jaw. "Yep, where you gonna find her? There ain't no young women in our little town. Sweet's got cowboys and sodbusters, but unless you're able to see something I can't see, then where exactly you goin' to find this bride? If I was you, I wouldn't be too hasty in turning her away."

"He's right. This might be your last chance, Sam."

"Yer brother might be right." Chauncey grinned and then, without another word, he turned Tidbit and tromped off down the road, whistling as he went.

He watched the old man riding away then he shot Gil a glare. "Don't you have chores to tend to?"

Gil huffed an exasperated breath. "Don't let her get away. Remember, I benefit from this too."

"If you know what's good for you, then you'd better get back to work. This is my life this matchmaker is playing with and I'll not have it."

"Fine." Gil spun and stomped off, his shoulders stiff.

Sam reread the letter.

How had this happened? Who was it who thought

he needed a wife? It was true he'd been thinking about the idea of a wife but then he'd talk himself out of it. But to think that someone in town had taken it upon themselves to send for a wife for him was unacceptable.

He wasn't a charity case and he could make his own decisions. He thought about what Chauncey had pointed out and it was true; he did get lonesome out here. His brother lived across the pasture in his small cabin and worked the ranch right along beside him, so he had company.

A wife was different, though, and the thought churned inside him. *A wife would be nice.*

But not a mail-order bride who someone else had picked out for him. Nope, he wasn't standing for that. He would go to town and he would send the poor woman back where she came from. And if he had to resort to sending for his own mail-order bride, he would. But he would be in control of who he sent for and not some anonymous matchmaker.

Who was the matchmaker anyway? There was speculation that the church ladies might be responsible.

He hadn't really given it much thought, until now, because he'd had no idea he would be a target.

Later, as he lay in bed that night, tired and worn out from building a fence and digging out the creek, he wondered about the woman he would meet at the stage in the morning.

The woman who had braved the rugged trip across Texas to marry a stranger.

The woman he was going to turn away. The thought dug at him.

CHAPTER TWO

Megan Scott stepped out of the stagecoach feeling as if she had ridden across the Texas landscape in an open-air carriage during a dust storm. The stagecoach hadn't been much protection from the grit and grime of the Texas Panhandle. She had traveled from St. Louis and it had been long and the travel had been hard. Though she had closed the flaps during a sandstorm across the plains, sand had coated everything. She was pretty grimy and felt awful at the thought of meeting the man who would be her groom, her husband, without having had a proper bath to get rid of all the layers of dirt on her. She was feeling very self-conscious.

Trying not to worry, she glanced around at the town. It wasn't bad, not compared to some she'd traveled through to get here. Many had been little more than dust bowls, with one or two buildings—and one of those being a saloon most of the time. Several times when she'd gotten off the stagecoach to use the facilities, she'd prayed that no drunks would bother her before she could get back inside the stagecoach. She'd dealt with enough of those back home. Her thoughts turned to her stepfather and she cringed. How her poor mother, Esther, had never really known the true colors of the man she'd married still baffled Megan. Megan had seen through Glen Carter the instant her mother brought him home two years earlier. She'd realized too clearly that her mother had made a huge mistake.

Then again, what was her mother to do after they'd lost Megan's sweet father in an accident at the mill? When his boss had eventually come to their rescue by offering her pretty mother his hand in marriage, Esther had believed it was a way to provide for her daughter. And so she had married him, despite Megan repeatedly begging her not to. But her mother wasn't in the best of health, had always been delicate, and she worried what would become of Megan. Pushing those thoughts away, she focused more closely on the town.

A Sweet's Mercantile was across the street and beside it, Sweet Treats Bakery. There were other stores along the boardwalk but it was the bakery that drew her attention. Men stood around outside, and there were also a few ladies at the door. They were all watching the stage. She wondered whether they were expecting someone on the stage. But there was no one but her traveling this section.

"Miss, did you hear? This is your stop. Sweet, Texas."

Startled from her thoughts, Megan inhaled a sharp breath and stared at the rough old stagecoach driver. "Thank you. I was just taking it in. Is everything named Sweet?"

His bushy brows dipped over confused eyes. "A few things. But the Sweet Treats Bakery is new. If I was you, I'd get over thar real quick and get some of their cherry scones. Are you gonna be okay?"

"Yes, I'm fine. Thank you for getting me here and for unloading my bags. I must admit, I'm not sad that I won't be riding on the stagecoach anymore. And to think, you ride up there on the top of that thing the whole way. I can't even imagine."

The old stagecoach driver laughed gruffly. "I been doin' this a long time and I've got used to it. But you see, this old grizzly beard and this old grizzly mustache keeps a lot of the dirt out of my mouth. You ain't got that option."

As he climbed up top, she scanned the street for any sign of her groom. Her thoughts darted back to her worrying about what kind of man he might be. After her mother died, leaving Megan devastated once more, she'd been eighteen and forced to live alone with her stepfather for a short while. But, fearing that her mother's health was worsening, she had taken her future into her own hands. Fearing if she were left alone with her stepfather eventually that things might not go well for her, she'd applied to become a mail-order bride. At least she had some choice in who she would marry or allow to touch her.

And she'd been right to worry because once her mother was buried, her stepfather turned his sights on her with his plans to marry her to his older partner. Fortunately, before he was able to force her, the train ticket had arrived that would take her to Sweet, Texas and her groom.

But, where was he?

Sick at heart and grieving, she prayed that the man she had opted to marry instead of facing the fate her stepfather had planned for her was as nice as his letters had sounded.

But most of all, she prayed he was responsible and strong enough to help her if or when her stepfather came after her. Surely a rancher would be strong. Working the land and livestock, she had assumed, would make him both strong and responsible. And maybe kind, because once he knew her story maybe he would naturally want to defend her. To keep her as his own. She hoped so. Prayed it would be so.

She had pluck and wanted to think she could take

care of herself, but she wasn't going to lie to herself. She knew she needed help if she were going to resist her stepfather from trying to force her to go back with him. She had a small hope that he couldn't take her back but she wasn't taking any chances and had chosen Sam McKay specifically.

She saw an old man with a mule tied to a hitching post not too far away and the old man grinned at her then spat a string of tobacco. She cringed and wasn't sure whether she should smile back or not. She was trying to decide this when a large man came out of the door of the Wiggins' Feed Store. At least it wasn't named Sweet's Feed Store.

"Miss," the man said. "Welcome to Sweet, Texas."

His smile was so genuine that it eased her nerves. He was balding, very large, and something about him reassured her that things might just be fine if everyone in this frontier town was half as welcoming as he was.

"Thank you."

"I'm Big John Wiggins, owner of the feed store. You look like you're looking for someone. And not

Chauncey." He frowned at the tobacco-spitting man, who grinned again but kept on standing where he was as if he were waiting on something.

Megan pulled her gaze off the strange older man and smiled at Mr. Wiggins. "It's nice to meet you. I'm Megan Scott and, well," she hesitated, a bit uncomfortable about telling the world she was a mail-order bride. "I'm waiting on my fiancé," she said, more comfortable with this than the other.

"I knew it," Chauncey exclaimed, slapped his leg and broke into a little jig right there in the street.

"Chauncey, why don't you go grab a scone on me at the bakery." Mr. Wiggins smiled at her. "Well, who might the lucky man be? I'll tell you if I've seen him in town today."

"Mr. Sam McKay." She inhaled, full of hope that his reaction would be reassuring. And blessed be the Lord, it was.

He smiled and his eyes twinkled. "Well, that is mighty fine. Mighty fine indeed. Sam is a lucky man and a good man. So that makes you equally as lucky. Congratulations. When will the nuptials be?"

Her mind went blank for a moment because of the immense relief that swept over her like a thunderstorm on a hot day. "I'm not certain. I'll leave that detail up to him."

"He's a smart man, I'm sure it will be soon. Would you like to wait inside the feed store?"

She glanced around, feeling apprehensive about his lateness. "Thank you but I'll wait here. I'm sure he'll be here soon."

"You're all set, little missy," the stagecoach driver said.

"Thank you."

"You listen up. I dropped another couple of the mail-order brides off here and I think they are doing real nice in their new lives. But, that ain't always the case. If you see you need a ride somewhere else any time, you jest be waiting here when my route comes through and I'll deliver you there safe and sound...a little dusty maybe, but I'll get you thar. I promise."

Her heart clenched. "Oh, Ulis. Thank you for your kindness but I'm sure I'll be just fine. You've been wonderful."

He blushed. "I aim to help. I'm hoping this is a good place fer you. But don't ferget what I said."

Touched, she couldn't help it as she placed a hand on his dusty arm and gave it a gentle squeeze. "Thank you. You're a blessing."

He paused, looking a bit astonished, but then he patted her arm, grinned and he sprang up the steps with amazing agility, given his age. Once he was perched on his seat, he tipped his dusty hat at her and then set the horses in motion. No other passengers had been waiting to board and no others had been on it with her, but she knew he had people to pick up and mail to deliver. She watched him head out and her heart clenched. Oh, how she hoped she didn't need his help in the future, but his kindness was reassuring.

A woman hurried from the bakery, waving at the stage. He pulled up as the lady waved a box at the man.

"You must have some scones," the older lady said, beaming as she held the box up to the nice driver.

"Thank you, ma'am. This will truly be a delight. I've had a hankering for more of your scones ever since you gave me a box on my last trip to town."

"Good. We're glad you enjoyed it. Please spread the word with all your passengers. We are trying to build a reputation across all the territories."

"I'll be glad to do that." The driver took a scone from the box and bit into it. "I don't get many treats like this, ma'am."

Even from this distance, she saw the look of pure joy on his scraggly face.

The older woman smiled up at him and looked satisfied. "Good. Now you take care out there on your travels." She stepped back and got out of his way. But as he took off, the older lady came in their direction instead of going back to the other side of the road to the bakery.

"That was nice of him to offer to take care of you," Mr. Wiggins said, his words reminding her that he was still standing a few feet away.

"Oh, yes, it was. He and you have both been kind to me." She didn't add that she wasn't used to that. She had been forced for the last few years to be on her guard since she had suspected many men had not-sonoble ideas about her after her father died. "I can only hope…" She let her words trail off, not having planned to voice her fears.

Big John Wiggins looked sympathetic. "Stop your worrying. If it's Sam McKay who's put those worry lines around your pretty eyes, then you can relax. Sam's a good man. A little set in his ways, but good nonetheless. I'm sure he'll be riding up any minute now. You can count on that."

"Sam McKay?" the older woman asked as she reached them. "Is that who you've come to meet?"

"Yes," Megan said.

"Afternoon, Mrs. Mulberry. This is Miss Megan Scott and she's here to marry Sam."

Excitement erupted on the older lady's face. "I do declare, this is marvelous. It is so nice to meet you. We were curious over at the bakery and I couldn't help coming over to welcome you to town and to find out if what Chauncey had told us this morning was true. It is a delight to have another mail-order bride in our town."

"Chauncey?" She looked toward the tobacco-spitting man, who was now leaning against the hitching post, grinning.

"Yes, he stopped by and told us he had delivered a letter to him yesterday, at Mr. Wiggins's request, and that Sam was the newest bachelor to get notice he had a mail-order bride coming. Gabby and Lucy will be thrilled. They are our other two brides." She spun and waved at the two ladies at the bakery, who clapped their hands in obvious delight; then they turned and rushed back into the bakery. "They would come and meet you but we had cookies ready to come out of the oven. So, I must rush back to help but we are thrilled and Sam is a wonderful man. We will see you soon. This is just wonderful news. Wonderful."

Megan watched the woman hustle back across the road and then, feeling slightly overwhelmed, looked from Chauncey to Mr. Wiggins. Megan caught the way the big man's gaze darted out, searching the surrounding area before returning to her. Surely if this kind man and Mrs. Mulberry said her intended was a nice man, it must be true. Surely, he didn't have the town deceived as her stepfather had those around him.

Suddenly his smile widened. "There he is now. See, I told you not to worry,"

Her gaze followed his. She very nearly gasped out loud as the best-looking man she'd ever seen rode toward them on a wheat-toned horse with a pale mane. Everything around her faded as she studied him. The cowboy's eyes were shielded by the hat he wore, but the sun glinted off them just enough for her to see the flash of white as his gaze found her. A shiver of awareness raced down her spine and a tingle settled deep in her stomach as her nerves danced.

Oh my. She hadn't expected his dark good looks. But if she'd hoped her groom would be strong, then her hopes were realized, because the man had broad shoulders and an intense expression that would send fear, or should send fear, through any man who crossed him. She knew the dandy that her stepfather was would, or should, take one look at Sam McKay and turn tail and run. The thought struck her that maybe she should do the same.

There was nothing weak about this man. Her knees were weak, but he wasn't and she would stake her last dollar on it.

Her breath was shaky as she swallowed the huge lump that clogged her windpipe.

"Are you okay?" Big John's worried voice penetrated her mangled thoughts.

"Fine. I'm fine," she muttered, hearing the croak of her words from the dryness in her mouth. For a moment, she thought she heard a chuckle from the big man. But when she glanced at him, he looked about as serious as a man meeting his maker.

What was she thinking? She squared her shoulders and told herself to act normal. And not get her hopes up. He barely had the horse stopped before he swung out of the saddle and stood before her.

She gasped and stepped back, never having seen a man so confident in his physical prowess. Her mouth went dry as his gaze locked on hers. Her brain muddled.

His eyes narrowed, deep indigo-blue eyes that held the storms of a summer sky within their depths. He had amazing eyes.

"Are you Megan Scott?"

She nodded then realized she hadn't actually spoken. "Yes," she said, startled by the breathy way her words came out. She'd never, ever heard that sound in her voice before. She tried to sound normal as she asked, "Are you Mr. Sam McKay?"

He swept his hat from his head and held it over his heart. "I am."

They continued to stare at each other as silence filled the expanse between them. Her heartbeat thumped out the seconds as his amazing eyes seemed to see right through her.

"I guess you're here to get married?"

His question registered as odd from the man who had sent for her. She nodded, wishing her heart would calm down so that her breathing would settle down.

Before he answered, Big John acknowledged him. "Sam, how are you today?" His voice filled the looming void of uncomfortableness spreading like a prairie fire.

"I've had less complicated days, Big John."

The older man hitched a brow. "I'd say meeting your bride-to-be would be a good day?"

Sam's gaze narrowed. "Under normal circumstances, that'd be true. But this is less than normal."

She caught the way his eyes narrowed and felt the sting of his words.

Big John crossed his arms. "Meaning what?"

Trepidation filled Megan's soul. *He had changed his mind about sending for her.*

Heat crept up her collar as her groom-to-be's gaze shifted to her and she thought she saw his skin turn a tinge of red beneath his dark tan. His tan, golden brown from the sun, she assumed. Her pale skin didn't do as good a job hiding the pink she knew she was and hated that he could see he'd just struck a nerve. Despite the awkwardness of the situation, the man intrigued her. Still, the question suddenly hung in the air like the threat of a thunderstorm: was he, or was he not, happy she was here?

He cleared his throat and those eyes held hers, as if weighing what his options were. She refused to look away. Refused to let him think she couldn't handle the outcome of her situation. But her heart thundered and her entire body felt weak with worry.

What if he didn't want her? Had changed his mind and wanted to send her back on the stage the way she'd come?

The stagecoach driver had said these things happened. But she had not dreamt it could happen to her. *Had she been that foolish? Or that desperate?*

Desperate—that was the easy answer and it was the truth.

This man held the key to helping her make a new life.

"Is there some kind of problem?" she asked, indignant and determined not to let the man get off lightly if he was choosing to back out of their agreement. Maybe he had been expecting someone prettier, or even beautiful. Neither terms would describe her.

Though she was passing in the looks department, she had no illusions that there were far prettier women in the world for a man to wed. Especially with there being so many women looking for a mate through the mail-order bride classifieds these days. The question hung in the air between them as they stared at each other. She was about to grit her teeth to nubs worrying when Mr. Wiggins cleared his throat loudly, causing Sam to obviously realize he hadn't answered the question.

"No." His eyes flared and his shoulders pulled back, showing the outline of his hard form beneath his cotton shirt. "I just left the preacher's and he said he'd marry us if that was what you still wanted when you arrived. He's waiting back at the house if you're sure that's what you want," he repeated, as if maybe she hadn't heard him the first time.

"I'm ready," she said hastily. She needed to be married as fast as she could because she had no idea how soon her stepfather was going to come following her. If she risked putting it off too long, he might be able to force her back.

Relief nearly melted her legs from beneath her. "I came here to get married and I'm not backing out now. And if we're going to your place, then I need to be married."

He nodded. "Okay then. I need to go to the stable

and rent a wagon. If you wait here, I'll be back."

"Can I go with you?" she said hurriedly, then blushed when his brow quirked. "I, I don't want to stand here," she explained. Her nerves clanged together.

"If you don't mind walking, then that'll be fine."

"I don't mind at all. I've been riding on that stage long enough that a walk sounds wonderful."

"Then you're welcome to walk. Big John, would you mind keeping an eye on her bags?"

Mr. Wiggins grinned from ear to ear. "I'll keep watch on her bags and I'll watch over your horse, too. You go tend to your business."

Sam nodded. "Much obliged."

And then he started walking in determined strides across the street, as if he'd forgotten she was walking with him.

Megan hurried to catch up, gathering her lavender skirts up so they wouldn't drag in the dirt. She wondered how old he was as she watched his long strides, noting his trim, fit form. She thought he might be somewhere between five to ten years older than her.

It was a nice age difference. Much better than the nearly thirty years' difference between her and her stepfather's partner. The very idea that her stepfather had planned to marry her off to his partner in order to better himself in the eyes of his business partner still caused her stomach to revolt.

Trying to find something to talk about, she offered, "I'm anxious to see the ranch. I can only imagine how beautiful it must be. Still, I imagine it might get lonesome out there."

He shot her a glance over his shoulder and immediately slowed, obviously realizing she was practically running to keep up with him.

"Yes, it is beautiful and lonesome. My brother Gil works with me but he's not always the best company and after we spend all day long together, we can get on each other's nerves right bad. It will sure be nice having someone else to talk to and real nice to have a clean house and cooked meals. I'm glad you can cook?"

"I'm glad I can help. But if you need me to bring food out to you in the pastures, I don't know how to ride a horse. But I'm sure I can learn."

"We'll worry about that later. I'll help you and in the meantime, you'll learn to use a buggy. I want you to know how to get around. You'll be too far out to have to rely on walking. And if something were to happen to me or even me and Gil, you will need to be able to get to town on your own."

He was a considerate man, she decided, and was very thankful for that. This entire situation was uncomfortable but at least she had that to be grateful for. And right now, she'd take whatever she could get.

When they reached the church, she was relieved to see the handsome preacher standing beside the door. He was much younger than she'd anticipated and there was a very pretty lady next to him.

She smiled brightly and hurried forward toward Megan. "Hello, I'm Gabby and I'm so glad to meet you. I'm one of the partners at the bakery and was a mail-order bride too. This is my husband, Pastor Andrews. He is going to officiate your wedding. When Mrs. Mulberry confirmed our hopes earlier, we were so excited. Then my husband came to the bakery and said he needed me to be a witness. Which I'm thrilled to do. I've been in your shoes myself and know the nerves that can be twisting inside you. Maybe it will comfort you to have someone who understands standing beside you as you and Sam say your vows."

"Yes, thank you." Megan was taken by surprise by Gabby Andrews's fast talking and the fact that she, too, had been a mail-order bride. She saw the way Gabby looked at Sam, as if she were thrilled for him to be getting married. He looked uncomfortable about the entire exchange.

Gabby patted his arm. "Don't look so alarmed, Sam. Everything is turning out wonderfully."

Megan deemed her a very nice person and it was reassuring to know that she had been a mail-order bride too. "Thank you so much for being here. I'm a little nervous." She wasn't sure whether it was okay to admit that and slid a glance at Sam, who ran a finger along the neckline of his shirt collar, looking suddenly nervous himself.

"It's very okay to be nervous." Pastor Andrews stepped up and held out his hand. "If for some reason you're too nervous and want to wait a few days, then we would be happy to offer a place for you to stay. We have an extra room here at the parsonage and you are welcome to use it for a few days."

She didn't want to wait. Didn't need to risk waiting. Sam's expression was suddenly full of…well, she wasn't sure what it was full of. Maybe consternation. Or anger? Frustration maybe?

"It's calving season and I'm building fences, too. If I do this, it would be really hard to come into town every day to visit. And I've decided to go along with this scheme today but if I put it off, I might decide not to go through with it."

She stared at him. "What do you mean, you're going along with this scheme?"

He sighed. "To be honest, I didn't decide to send for a mail-order bride."

She gasped. "You didn't?"

He looked from Gabby and the pastor, who both looked apologetically at her.

Sam sighed heavily. "No, I didn't. It seems the pastor and also the sheriff can vouch for this, that we have someone in Sweet who is sending for mail-order brides for the men. I'm the latest to be surprised by the information at the last minute. You are the third young lady to get off that stage who the mystery matchmaker sent for."

"I was number two," Gabby said. "Lucy, who is married to the sheriff, was the first."

Gabby couldn't believe her ears. "But…you wrote me letters."

"Not me. But, I decided on the ride to town that I do need a wife. And it looks like the preacher and the sheriff have done well, so I decided to go along with it. I only found out yesterday that you would be getting off that stage and expecting me."

Her face grew tight with embarrassment. "But—"

"It's not your fault. At first, I was aggravated about it. But then I realized I don't have a wife right now because I don't have time to come to town and court someone. And I won't have any time for a while yet. So, if we don't get married today, then you'll have to wait in town until I can make time again to come see you. It would be more convenient and since that's what the marriage would be I don't see why we should wait."

A marriage of convenience. Not exactly all she was hoping for the marriage to be but she wasn't in any position to make demands. She was deciding how to proceed when he continued-

"I need someone who can cook and clean and do laundry. That would help me out tremendously. If I'd have sent the letter myself that's what I would have been looking for in a bride."

"What about children?" she asked, struggling not to be disappointed that her being here wasn't his idea or that he very well might not want children. No matter what she couldn't dwell on these things because she needed to be married now. She had no time to wait. If her stepfather came looking for her it was the only thing that might stop him from taking her back with him.

His gaze locked onto hers and she had to look away as her cheeks heated.

"It's a hard land out here. I'm not looking for a family."

His words were like a nail to her heart. She wanted to cry out and say she wanted children but then he might not want to marry her, so instead she said, "I see. Fine, I'm ready to marry now. I'm disappointed that we didn't actually correspond but it was only one letter and then the letter you sent the train tickets for me to use if I wanted to. It was perfect timing for me."

"Then, let's get going. I thought we would do the service right there at the altar inside the church."

And so they entered the church. A mixture of relief and trepidation washed over her as she looked to Gabby. She and the pastor were both all smiles as they turned and led the way into the church and then down to the altar of the small, pretty church with its dark wood, tall ceiling, and well-cared-for wooden pews. She stood before the altar and looked at Sam. He was so handsome and he seemed good. She could only pray that he was all that he seemed.

Sam smiled at her as if to reassure her of any trepidation that might be filling her. He was a very serious person, she thought, and the smile was probably out of character for him and yet he'd smiled.

She told herself that it was his being a responsible man was exactly what she needed. And as the preacher started the ceremony, she concentrated on the fact that he was a responsible, handsome man and he would protect her.

~ ~ ~

"I now pronounce you husband and wife. Sam, you may kiss your bride."

Sam shot the pastor a glare then quickly blinked it away. He had made it through the ceremony but hadn't been thinking about kissing her. This was a practical marriage. He'd made the decision on the way into town, realizing he needed a wife and she had traveled this far because she wanted or needed a husband. It only made sense that they marry. He'd talked to the preacher about it and set everything up before heading to the stage stop. But when he'd spotted her standing there with Big John Wiggins, he'd been thrown off-balance. Her eyes had been huge as they met his and though she tried to hide it, she'd seemed very vulnerable in that moment. He'd wanted nothing more than to protect her. He'd been fighting to keep himself focused on the practical notion of the marriage but now, he was supposed to kiss her. His chest felt as if it had a thousand mules trying to kick their way out as he thought about kissing her soft, pink lips.

Pastor Andrews stared at him. "You may kiss your bride," he repeated and then nodded toward Megan.

Swallowing hard, Sam looked at Megan. She looked at him with that vulnerable expression, as if she expected him to run away and leave her standing at the altar. But almost defiantly, she lifted her chin in what he felt was her attempt to appear strong. His mouth had gone bone dry and his chest was beginning to hurt from the mule attack, so he did the only thing he could do: he leaned forward and kissed her rosy pink lips. She gasped softly as their lips touched and Sam felt as if his world had started spinning. He pulled back, startled by the sensations racing over him.

Fighting an overwhelming want to pull her into his arms and kiss her again, he stepped back. "We better go now if we're going to make it home before dark. I still have calves to feed."

"Okay, whatever you think," she said, her voice breathless. "I'm ready."

And that was the problem, he realized too late. *She might be ready, but was he?*

~ ~ ~

Megan stood there, staring at her husband. Her thoughts repeated everything about the moment that she'd heard the pastor say Sam could kiss his bride. He'd stared at her and his brows dipped; her heart had thundered like one of the fierce prairie storms the stagecoach had been caught up in when they were crossing the panhandle. She hadn't thought about the fact that he was going to kiss her at the end of the ceremony.

She had hoped for a few days to adjust to being his bride. But then, as he stepped forward and dipped his head to hers, instantly her weak knees had gone weaker as his lips touched hers. It felt as if a lightning bolt hit her. When he'd suddenly pulled away, she'd thought he'd looked slightly dazed, as dazed as she felt. She told him she was ready to head home and then they thanked Gabby and the pastor.

Her lips still tingled as she followed Sam, her husband, to the door of the church. She told herself to get hold of her senses but the feel of his gentle kiss was like nothing she'd ever experienced before. *Her first kiss.*

When they reached the buggy, Gabby wrapped an arm around Megan's waist and gave her a hug as if they had been friends forever.

"We're here if you need anything. I'll try to get out soon with some of the ladies of town to give you a housewarming. We are so glad for you." She leaned in close so only Megan could hear her. "Sam is a wonderful man and if I had been this matchmaker who has been matching people up, Sam would have been my next choice on the list. He's a quiet, serious man and seems like he would make a good husband. I think you will be a blessing in his life and he in yours."

Megan hoped so. He was being a blessing to her just by marrying her. "I'm going to give it my best."

And she was. She was so grateful for having found a man who seemed to have such a good reputation when back home she had such an unsavory fate waiting for her. He or anyone might never know how much this marriage meant to her. She hoped they didn't ever need to know. Hoped her stepfather didn't come looking for her.

Gabby smiled. "I'm so glad." She moved to stand by her husband.

Pastor Andrews shook Sam's hand. "We'll be saying prayers for you two." He wrapped his arm around his wife's shoulders and they watched as Sam held his hand out for Megan's.

She slipped hers into his and felt a tingle slip along her fingertips and up her arm as he held her hand. Feeling slightly off-center, she stepped up into the buggy and settled into the seat.

He climbed up, sat beside her and took the reins. "Ready?"

"Yes." She breathed a sigh of relief as the buggy finally moved forward. The sense of relief grew as they headed out of town. *She was safe.* Or at least as safe as she could possibly be. And with any luck and a few prayers, maybe her stepfather would stay in St. Louis and not come this direction.

And as she studied her new husband's profile, she couldn't help but feel a sense of excitement on top of her relief.

CHAPTER THREE

The sun was hot as they traveled but it was a gorgeous day as the road wound through the countryside. Texas was a land of many landscapes, she realized. On the trip out, the stage had passed through flat, dry country with tumbleweeds rolling everywhere and land that dropped into canyons and then more vast nothingness for days. The dust and dirt was almost unbearable and she'd been thankful when the land had changed to sage and smaller rock-covered hills and cliffs but there were trees. Small ugly trees that one of the men who had traveled a short way with them had told her were called mesquite trees. But at least they were green and gave something other than dirt to look at as the miles rolled by. When the land had shifted to green pastures and large oaks spanning the landscape and she saw brooks and creeks, she'd felt almost giddy with relief. This land seemed more fertile and she felt that life here at least wouldn't seem so harsh.

Now, as she drove along with Sam, he informed her who lived in the ranches and homes they passed. The farther out they went, the fewer and fewer homes, ranches, and farms there were.

"How far out do you live?" She took her eyes from the horizon and looked at her husband's handsome profile. Unexpected butterflies fluttered inside her chest, or maybe it was just nerves as she thought about the new life ahead of her. Back home, she'd lived on pins and needles for ages and only now was she realizing just how stressful it had been.

He looked at her and his gaze seemed to bore into hers. "It's a good four-hour drive in a buggy. It can be made in three hours on horseback. Sooner if you ride hard. We'll stop at a stream about midway and let the horses get a drink and rest. I packed a basket of food so we can take a break and eat. And Mrs. Mulberry sent along one of her special care boxes, which will be really good, because she makes the most wonderful treats in her bakery. She, Gabby Andrews, and Essie Jane Tate opened a bakery not too long ago and it's been real nice. It's a blessing to us bachelors who don't have time to bake treats. I'm really looking forward to some home-cooked meals—you do cook, right?"

"I do cook. And I bake, but I'm not sure it'll be as good as whatever you've got in those boxes. I can learn, though. Gabby said I could ask for her help anytime, so if you don't like my cooking maybe I can go to town and she or these other two ladies could teach me to make some things you really enjoy."

"I'm sure you'll make something I'll love."

A thrill went through her at the thought of making something that pleased him. It was normal to want to please her husband, even if she hadn't known him for very long. The fact that he was willing to take her on was enough to make her want to do something that pleased him. And there was the thought that if she pleased him maybe eventually he might want more of the marriage. Maybe he might want children. Maybe when they got to know each other better. "So tell me how you came to own this ranch."

He studied the horizon. "My family settled here when I was a teen. It was a great adventure for me and Gil. But after my mom and dad got sick and we lost them I learned how rough it is out here and I worried about bringing a wife this far out. Though, my mother wasn't the healthiest woman to begin with, and my dad just worked himself down. As you can see, I worried about bringing someone out here when so many close to me haven't been able to survive."

"I'm pretty healthy. Honestly, I've never been sick much. I think that I've got a pretty strong constitution."

He smiled at her. "Good, because I hope to have a wife who can grow old with me. I think there's a satisfaction that you get when you accomplish something together."

She stared at him, his words seeping through her like golden sunlight. "That sounds lovely."

His lips curved slightly, almost a smile as his

serious eyes held hers. "Plus, I'd hate to bring you all the way out here and have something happen to you. I'd feel terrible about that."

"Don't worry about me. Technically, you didn't bring me out here. To be honest, you're doing me a big favor letting me come out here. I needed to leave St. Louis."

"Why did you want to be a mail-order bride? I'm assuming there was a reason."

She fiddled with her dress and decided to be frank. "My mother passed away and my stepfather wanted to marry me to his partner to help business relations. His partner is old enough to be my father. I couldn't tolerate the idea of marrying him. My mother was ill for some time and suspected this might be his plan, so before she died, she told me I needed to get out. That's when I decided to reply to the letter I saw in the paper. I hope that it doesn't make you upset that I came here under those circumstances." She had watched his expression darken as she talked and it worried her.

"No, not at all. I'm glad you got out. Your stepfather sounds like a louse. I'm assuming he doesn't know where you are?"

Relieved by his words, she shook her head.

"Good. I'm glad I could help somehow or at least whoever this matchmaker is in town helped you."

"You helped me too, by agreeing to this marriage after being manipulated by the matchmaker." It was so true. "I'm very grateful."

"Well, it might be only a marriage of convenience but at least we'll both benefit."

His words hung between them again, and she realized that she should probably be relieved that he had no expectations of her other than being a housekeeper than a wife. But instead of relief she felt empty. She had lost her mother, and her father so long ago, and she realized that she had given up the prospect of ever knowing love by becoming a mail-order bride. She suddenly missed her mother so much.

~ ~ ~

Megan gazed at her new surroundings, her new home. Her nerves rattled inside her as she passed by Sam. He had opened the front door and then stepped back to let her pass. As she did, her elbow brushed his midriff. She felt the hardness of his stomach and instantly was reminded that this man was her husband. Butterflies fluttered through her and she quickly stepped farther into the room, putting distance between them. She took in the fireplace on the left of the kitchen area and the neat sitting area before it. A chair with soft cushions sat beside a settee that looked like something a woman would have chosen. His mother maybe. The kitchen table sat in the center of the room. The room had possibilities and she wondered whether he would mind if she rearranged it for a more pleasing effect. She would ask him later but for now she was glad to see that it was pleasant and not a shack that she was moving into.

Her eyes paused on the door across from the fireplace. *Was that the bedroom?* As if in answer, Sam strode silently past her into that room and she followed. She paused in the doorway. The large bed was the focal point of the room. There was a pretty quilt on top, done in cream and a rich burgundy. There were pretty curtains hanging on the window to match the burgundy in the quilts. They looked slightly worn but she could tell they had once been very pretty. And there was an armoire against the wall. And a cane-backed chair next to it. And then, in the other corner, there was a wash stand and a rug on the floor that looked as if it might have been handmade with the materials that matched the room.

"The room is lovely. Did you decorate?"

"My mother. This was my parents' room until they died and then I took it. But if you want to change anything, you can. My mother was a handy seamstress and really enjoyed making things. But that was a long time ago so you may want to make changes. There are some other things she made and more material in the hayloft of the barn. Or, I can take you to the mercantile and you can get what you need there."

"Thank you. I will enjoy looking through the things your mother made. It sounds like she and I had something in common. I really enjoy sewing myself. And I love looking at and learning the stitches that others have used. That quilt is beautiful. Although I'm here to cook, so I will only do things like that whenever you don't need me cooking or cleaning."

His brow furled. He looked perplexed as he tugged his hat from his head. Holding it between his hands, he studied her. "You won't be doing that all the time. You can do what you want. I mean, you're my wife."

Her nerves were not helping because he was so good-looking and she found him very pleasing to her eyes. When she looked at him, she saw all the things that she wanted in a man…in a husband. In the father of her children. She pushed the thoughts away.

Maybe with time, she would become bold enough to ask whether he could give her a baby. But not now. Now she would make him glad to have her here to cook for him. For now she wanted to make sure he didn't have any reason to regret marrying her. "Okay." She took a deep breath. "If you'll be so kind as to show me where the water is so I can wash up before I start supper?"

He nodded. "I'll bring some in to you." He moved past her and she watched as he left the room and closed the door behind him.

She sighed, her hand pressing her ribs as the butterflies had erupted when he'd passed her and her knees felt weak. *What was wrong with her?*

She was here, she was safe, and her new life was starting off pleasantly. *Then what was troubling her suddenly?* Her mouth was dry as she studied the closed door. *It was this feeling of weakness that came over her every time he came near. What was she supposed to do about that?*

~ ~ ~

Sam set a pitcher of water on the floor beside the door then tapped on it and let Megan know it was there. Then, before she could open the door, he left the house and stomped across the yard to the barn and much-needed space to get some air. This having a wife was going to take some getting used to. He'd needed to let his new wife get used to her kitchen and he was actually looking forward to a good meal. The last thing he wanted to do was make her feel uncomfortable and mess up what could be a really good thing for him and Gil. Hot meals were not something to take lightly and that was precisely why he'd agreed to this.

That was what he needed to focus on.

Not how soft her lips looked or how pretty she was. Or how every time he looked at her, he had the overwhelming desire to pull her close and kiss her.

Nope, a hot meal was worth too much to mess up by frightening her with this need to kiss her. He and Gil worked such long hours, the last thing he wanted to do was cook when they came inside, so they ate a lot of beans and jerky. He was tired of beans and jerky and sometimes bacon or some other meat but their diets were pretty basic.

And that was a really sad reason to marry a complete stranger but that was the truth of it.

He hadn't expected to be attracted to her. This was going to really complicate things.

Trying to tend to business and not thoughts that were better left unthought at the moment, he carried some meat into the house from the cellar. She had changed into a light-blue dress that was simple but fit her well. Too well, as she looked very appealing in it. He showed her where he kept the supplies in a small cupboard at the end of the kitchen counter. It was then that he realized he really was low on supplies. He didn't have any vegetables because the raccoons had gotten into the garden while they were out on the range and eaten or destroyed everything. Not that he or Gil had taken time to cook many vegetables.

But he could buy some from the neighbors and made a note to do so when he carried her back into town to the store.

He hadn't lingered and she'd looked almost relieved that he had to go feed the horses before dinner.

Tulip, his milk cow, studied him from her stall as he entered the barn. He frowned. "Don't look at me like I've done something wrong. I'm just looking for somebody to help out around here. I don't need anything more."

Tulip's big brown eyes bore into him, and he got the feeling the cow didn't believe him. He wasn't sure he believed himself.

He heard footsteps and turned to see Gil rushing toward him. The boy rushed everywhere.

"Is she here?" Gil grinned like a kid rather than a twenty-year-old man. "Did you bring her?"

Sam nodded toward the house. "She's in there, cooking supper."

"Well, come on—"

"Hold on," Sam barked. "You're not going in there until she's done fixin' the meal."

Gil's brows dipped. "I can't wait. I can't believe we're gonna actually have some good food around here. Or that you actually brought her home. I expected you were gonna go back up there and send her packin'. But I have to admit, I'm proud of you. My stomach was needing something different than what we eat all the time. Those treats we get in town don't last near long enough."

Sam frowned. "If it was as awful as you say, then why haven't you said something before? Or married someone yourself?"

Gil gaped at him. "Sam, I didn't say I was desperate. I'm young, anyway. *You're* the one who's old. You're the one who needs a woman."

"Old? Watch who you're calling old. I'm not much older than you."

"You act a whole lot older. You're grumpy all the time and you stomp around like you're mad at the world. You don't talk that much, so maybe a woman being around will do you some good."

"Yeah, maybe," Sam grunted. "I'm not that old. Now, when you go in there, you show your manners. Don't go grabbing all the food and eating it up like you don't know what's what. Mama wouldn't want you forgetting what she tried to teach you."

Gil looked shocked. "I wouldn't do that. I don't want to hurt her feelings or anything like that. I'm glad she's here. I remember what I was taught. But don't you run her off. Is she cute?"

The question came out of nowhere and Sam coughed. "One minute we're talking about food and the next minute you're asking me if she's cute?"

"Well, is she?"

Sam swallowed hard and thought about the soft lines of her face, the pretty pink lips, and the gentle curves the blue dress showed off. "She's, um, yes, she's pretty."

Gil frowned and his brows slammed together. "You sure ain't saying it with very much enthusiasm. You'd think you'd be all excited that she's pretty and not twice your age…she isn't twice your age, is she?"

"No, she's not older. She's somewhere between your age and my age. And you're right, that is a benefit." Sam hadn't thought about the fact that some mail-order brides were known to lie about their age. "Still, this is only a business relationship. She's here to cook and to keep the house while we work to build this ranch. What she looks like doesn't matter. Doesn't matter at all."

Gil's eyes grew wide as wagon wheels and he cocked his head to one side as he stared at him. "You like her." He grinned and his eyes turned on like the flame of an oil lamp turning up to full flame.

Sam had to fight not to shift his weight and look all guilty. "I do not," he denied.

"You don't like your new wife?"

"I didn't say that. She's nice. But still, it would be

best to not let anything but business into this relationship. Anything else can make the situation complicated and it very well could be the thing that ruins it for everyone."

Gil didn't look convinced. "I don't know, big brother. You had me worried. I don't see why you wouldn't want to make this marriage a real marriage if you like her."

"Gil, why don't we just agree you mind your business and let me tend to my business? I married her to give her security and to get us some good meals. You should just be happy about that and stop pressuring me about all this other stuff. What's between me and my wife is between me and my wife."

Gil grinned at him. "Now that sounds more promising. Maybe you won't be of the 'just business' stuff soon. I can't wait to see her. I might just want to send off for a mail-order bride for myself. Since that matchmaker hasn't sent for one for me or my buddies."

"You aren't ready to get married."

"I might be."

Sam scowled. "Don't rush into anything."

Gil grinned. "I wouldn't but I think I have a new pastime—watching you squirm."

"Sam," a sweet, soft voice called.

Gil spun toward the sound and then spun back to him. "She sounds nice. Real nice. Let's go eat."

Sam fought to remain calm as he reached for his brother's arm. "I'm not kidding. You behave yourself in there and don't you do anything to embarrass our guest."

"Our guest? I was thinking since you married her that she's family now."

Sam let out a long, slow breath and let Gil go. "You're right. But watch yourself. I mean it."

"I plan to."

Sam followed Gil toward the house at a slower pace. His stomach growled and seemed to rumble all the way to his toes. The minute he entered the kitchen, he knew he was in trouble. It smelled like heaven. And she looked like an angel.

Gil stood beside Megan at the stove, looking completely smitten. Gil looked at him over Megan's head and he grinned. "Megan is nice, Sam. And she made us steak with biscuits and gravy. And apple dumplings."

"It smells great," Sam muttered, forgetting what else he was planning to say when Megan turned to look at him. His entire body responded the instant their eyes met.

It was everything he could do not to go to her and take her into his arms and thank her with a kiss for making him such a wonderful-smelling meal.

He was losing his mind.

CHAPTER FOUR

Megan settled in for the night after she cleaned the kitchen. She felt a sense of accomplishment having both men be so complimentary of the meal she prepared them. Their praise and obvious delight in having a good meal gave her a sense of pride. She especially enjoyed seeing the pleasure she brought to her new husband. He had been awkward at first but the minute he'd taken the first bite of her perfectly cooked biscuit, he'd looked as if he'd died and gone to heaven. It had been gratifying to watch him dig in after that and eat with gusto.

The man cleaned his plate and even had two dumplings. Gil did too. He was nice and talked the whole time he was eating. Sam, on the other hand, was a man of few words as he ate and listened. And when their gazes met, she felt weak and was glad she was sitting down.

After dinner, Gil had gone home and she wasn't sure what Sam was doing out in the barn. She found herself glancing out the window toward the barn, where a soft light glowed.

Weariness clung to her but she didn't want to go to bed and not at least tell him good night. She also wasn't sure where he was going to sleep. There was another room down the hall and even though he hadn't shown it to her, she wasn't sure whether he planned to sleep there or in the room with her. He was the one who insisted that this was a marriage of convenience. She was just about ready to give up and to go ahead and go to bed, because it had been such a long day for her, when he came back inside. He looked startled to see her.

He yanked his hat from his head and hung it on

the hat rack. "You're still up." His gaze raked down her before it swung to the kitchen. "The kitchen looks great but I thought you'd already be in bed. You have to be tired."

She had worked hard to make the kitchen sparkle and it had given her something to do while she waited on him. "I didn't know if you were through with me. I didn't want to just leave you without asking or at least saying good night."

He put his hands on his hips. "I should have told you to go ahead and go to bed before I went out to work on my harnesses. I wasn't thinking and I know you've had a very long day."

"It was. But it was also a good day. I just want to thank you for being who you said you were and for not misrepresenting yourself."

His brows met and she studied the darkness of them, realizing he had very nice brows. His eyes—she loved his eyes. They were unusual and… *What was she thinking?* She was just here for convenience.

"Remember, I did not write the letters. I didn't misrepresent or represent myself at all. Someone else sent those letters to you. But I'm glad that they found you. And that you're here and if there's one thing I can offer you, it is a safe place to be. I realized while I was working that you may have had hopes of more from this marriage when you agreed to come out here in your letters. If you want to we can leave that door open as we get to know each other."

Her heart jumped in her chest and she knew her expression had to show shocked elation at the same time. He wasn't completely closing up the possibility of them becoming truly man and wife and her have the possibility of becoming a mother. "That would be nice. But I understand if you don't want to commit to something like that right away. Well, I guess I'll go to bed. Where will you sleep?" She couldn't help asking the question.

He nodded toward the other room. "I'll sleep there. Good night."

Her gaze went to the door to his room and disappointment rocked through her. Her cheeks heated and she knew she was blushing. "Very well, good night." She spun and hurried to her room, closing the door behind her.

What must he think of her? He had to have seen the blush that came to her cheeks. They were married, after all. She took her gown from her bag and quickly got ready for bed. Once she slipped into bed, she lay there, wide awake despite her weariness. She felt safe here. Her thoughts went to Sam in the other room. Her hand moved to the spot beside her, where her husband should be sleeping. When she finally fell asleep, her thoughts were on her husband. And wishing he were lying there beside her.

~ ~ ~

Sam could not sleep. He lay in the bed and stared up at the ceiling. In the dim light of the lantern, he watched the shadows play across the exposed rafters. He wasn't happy as his thoughts went to the fact that this was his wedding night. It was his own fault considering he'd said it was a marriage of convenience that now his bride slept in one room and he in this one. It wasn't what he'd always hoped for but he'd let himself be roped into this situation and it served him right that he was now in a fix.

He had a very pretty wife, a wonderful cook, and from all accounts, a sweet wife. And he wasn't going to let himself do anything that might harm their arrangement. But he couldn't get the pretty blush that had colored her cheeks off his mind when she'd said it would be nice to make the marriage more when they knew each other better.

Or, could it have been worry that he misread as longing?

He was a man who hadn't had enough dealings with a woman to understand them. So asking himself these questions was useless.

But as he finally drifted off to sleep, it was with thoughts of his wife and how she'd felt in his arms as he'd kissed her at the wedding. He was going to have trouble not doing that again and he knew it.

~ ~ ~

Over the next couple of days, Megan wasn't sure what

to make of her new husband.

She woke each morning and fixed breakfast after not really sleeping well. Her thoughts had been focused on her husband in the other room. She couldn't help but be curious about him. He was so handsome. Even now her thoughts focused on him once more, wondering whether he wanted children. She wanted them but with this arrangement, there would not be any in her future. She was here to clean and cook and that was what she did. At least it gave her a way to release her building frustrations. They fell into a routine over that first week, with him coming in in the mornings and eating quickly before leaving. Gil came in a couple of mornings and though he tried to stay and talk—he was a very talkative young man— Sam would hurry him out quickly too. They had work to do. The evenings were the same: Sam would eat, and Gil would talk, and she would serve the meal and listen to Gil talk.

By the end of the week, the house sparkled and though it had been a little dusty when she arrived, there was no dust to be found now. The furniture had been oiled so that it gleamed and she was proud of what she'd done but Sam hadn't seemed to notice. He'd seemed preoccupied and distant. At the end of the week, five days after having arrived, she was starting to feel irritable. Sam barely looked at her? Barely talk to her? She hadn't expected that at all. And she really didn't know whether she could continue to go on this way. It had been the longest five days of her life.

What would it be like in five years? Or fifteen years? The thought was unbearable. Something had to change.

She thought of Gabby and longed to go to town and see her and meet the other women. Maybe they could give her some suggestions on how to make her husband pay attention to her. She decided at dinner that evening she would suggest or ask if maybe they could go into town for Sunday services. She was afraid it would be impossible considering they lived so far out of town, but they needed supplies, too, so maybe if they got up really early on Sunday morning and made the trip into town in time for the service, then they could spend the night and bring supplies home on

Monday. And she would have time to visit with the women.

Feeling hopeful, she fixed the beef stew with potatoes and waited for the men to come in from the pastures. When she saw them riding into the yard, her stomach swirled with hope. She watched through the window as they dismounted and took the horses into the barn to cool them down. She bit her lip as she waited. They washed up at the water pump, and she found herself watching closely as Sam removed his shirt and washed his muscled chest. She'd realized he did this on days when it had been really hot and now she was here at the window every evening, catching a glimpse of his strong torso.

She felt kind of odd and placed a hand on her stomach as she thought about his muscles and the feel of his arms around her. And when he turned to come to the house, she hurried from the window and busied herself putting plates on the table and filling the glasses with water.

"Hello," she said, when Sam entered the room. It always seemed smaller when he entered. When they sat down, she lifted the napkin she had over the cornbread, then filled bowls with the stew and placed them on the table. She'd found a tablecloth in the cupboard, probably something that had been their mother's, and she'd placed it on the table. She hoped to pick out a few pieces of material while in town so that she could make some curtains and a new tablecloth to add more color and a little of her own taste to the room as he had suggested. And she could use some of her time to make herself some new dresses too.

She didn't know anything about their finances, but Sam had said if she needed something she should ask. So, she would ask. She clasped her hands together and stood beside the table as their gazes locked.

Butterflies fluttered in her chest.

"It smells good in here." He moved to the table and took a chair.

"It sure does," Gil agreed, taking the chair across from Sam.

She barely heard Gil as she was thinking suddenly about Sam's bare chest. *Oh, she wished he would lock those strong arms around her again.*

Gil picked up a piece of cornbread. "I've been thinking about your good cooking all day long. We worked hard today and I am starving."

"Thank you, Gil. I tried to fix something I thought you and Sam might like."

"Are you okay?" Sam's gaze dug into hers.

"Yes, I'm fine." She sat down in her chair.

Sam thanked the Lord for their food and their many blessings, and then he and Gil dug into the food.

Sam paused, breaking a piece of cornbread. "Are you not hungry?"

"I am."

"You're not eating. And you look like you're scared or worried or sick. Are you sick?"

"No. I have something to ask you."

He set his cornbread down and placed his hands beside his plate, his palms flat on the table. "Okay. What do you want to ask?"

"I am here all day alone. And you hardly talk to me. And I need…" She paused, unable to go on. Her heart thundered in her chest so hard, she felt as though it were going to bust out and jump around on the table.

He looked suddenly guilty.

"You don't talk to Megan?" Gil asked, looking shocked.

Sam shot his little brother a look. "We talk. What do you need?" he asked quietly.

She decided now was not the moment to point out to him that he really didn't talk to her. "I was wondering if we could go to town. I need some supplies and some material for curtains and cushions and maybe a new dress. I was hoping we could go in early Sunday and attend church service, then come back on Monday with the supplies. I would love to see Gabby again and also the other ladies in town. Do you think that is possible?"

Tears suddenly pricked her eyes and she blinked them away. *What was wrong with her?* She refused to let herself feel weak and vulnerable as emotions welled up inside her. She had known what she was getting into when she came here, so just because she'd held out hope that she and her new husband might find love in their marriage of convenience, she was realizing that it was hopeless if he wouldn't spend any time with her.

"We can do that," he said quietly.

"That's great." Gil sounded as excited as Megan felt.

Her gaze flew to Sam's. She blinked really hard, trying to make the threatening tears evaporate. But one seeped from the corner of her eye and trailed down her cheek. Sam's gaze narrowed and his jaw tensed as she quickly dashed the dampness away with her fingertips. He laid his hand on hers. And she very nearly fainted.

CHAPTER FIVE

Guilt slammed into Sam as he stared at his wife. "Gil, get the buggy prepared for tomorrow before you leave for the night. We'll leave in the morning and spend two nights at the hotel. We'll leave after we feed the animals. We'll go into town for supplies and will get a couple rooms at the hotel for the night and will go to church on Sunday morning."

"I'll go do that now." Gil stood and started from the table but stopped and picked up another piece of cornbread. He grinned at her. "This is great. Thanks for another great meal. You're about the best cook I've ever known. If I get me a bride one day, I sure hope she can cook half as good as you."

His compliment touched her as she watched him head outside.

Sam's hand still covered hers on the table top and now his thumb caressed her skin. "I haven't been fair to you and I'm sorry."

Her gaze lifted from watching the motion of his thumb moving gently along the top of her hand. His touch caused her stomach to pull tightly and her heart to thunder. Looking up, she saw sincerity in his eyes. She was so flustered by his gentle touch that she couldn't speak and before she found her voice, he continued.

"I wasn't thinking about you being lonely and needing some conversation in the evening."

She was all too aware of his touch and the heat radiating from his fingertips, straight to the fluttery feeling in her stomach.

"I have things on my mind." His gaze burned into hers.

She couldn't look away. "Things? What things?"

He lifted a hand and cupped her jaw and she gasped very softly. His touch felt so nice. Just like what she had thought it might feel like. His work-roughened hand against her skin sent little sensations along her spine and she could have sat there and experienced it for the rest of her life. It was a crazy thought but she couldn't help it.

"Things like this…" He leaned forward and kissed her. His lips on hers were firm and yet gentle like their first kiss at their wedding but it went on longer and she sank into him. She knew that this was what she could experience for a lifetime. Her whole world spun; it was amazing and then suddenly, he pulled away. And then he stood. Her heart raced so wildly she couldn't think straight.

"I've got to go do chores in the barn but if you'll be ready in the morning, after breakfast, we'll load up and head for town. Be prepared to stay until Monday morning. And also, they'll probably be having a picnic afterward, so if you have something that we could take for the picnic, that will be good. But if not, we can go by the bakery and pick up one of their delicious pies.

Since we will be there for two days, it might be better if we do that."

He strode out the door and she just sat there. Her world was still spinning. Her husband had just kissed her and she wasn't sure what to think of it.

Touching her lips, she stared at the door he'd just closed behind him. And she felt a new ray of hope that maybe God was going to help this marriage turn into a real one.

~ ~ ~

Sam's knees were weak as he strode to the barn. He'd tried not to kiss her. Tried all week long not to want to kiss her. And it had been pure torture, sitting at that table with her each night and not be able to touch her. But tonight, when she'd cried, he'd thought his heart would break. He didn't like seeing her cry. And it had made him forget his determination to keep his heart out of this marriage and he'd kissed her.

And she'd kissed him back, setting lose a whole host of feelings through him.

Yes, it was time to go to town because he had some thinking to do. And maybe he needed to talk to the preacher when he got to town. He needed more advice.

Gil was just heading home when Sam reached the barn.

"I think you made a good decision to take Megan to town. She looked like she needs it. I don't know what to do about a crying female. Better you than me."

Sam frowned. "I didn't know what to do about it either."

Gil climbed into the saddle of his horse. "You looked like you did."

His little brother needed to get to town more often, Sam decided. Maybe they all needed to get away from the solitude of the ranch and around friends more often. He decided making it to church on Sundays could start being a normal thing. At least twice a month, if they couldn't make it every Sunday. Now that he had a woman in the house, it was his responsibility to make sure she had what she needed. And socializing some was part of that, he figured.

He'd liked the look of happiness that had colored her pretty face when he agreed to take her. His heart had lunged in his chest at the light that had leapt in her eyes.

He wanted to see more of that.

The next morning, as they rode toward town, he could feel the excitement radiating from Megan. He was feeling pretty happy, too, riding next to her. Their arms brushed each other and every time it happened, it sparked a flame inside him. He was definitely talking to the preacher about what he was feeling. The preacher had his own mail-order bride, so he would understand. Maybe he needed to talk to the sheriff, too.

Gil rode on his horse beside the buggy, on Megan's side. They'd decided to take the horse and the buggy because Gil had said he might want to do a little courting while he was in town. Sam hadn't minded being alone in the buggy with Megan.

"I'm glad you're here." Gil grinned at Megan. "You're going to enjoy today. The hotel's nice. I've eaten lunch there but never stayed in one of the rooms. Are me and you sharing one of the rooms, Sam?"

"Yes," Sam said gruffly. "I'm hoping they have one of those that join together. Me and you can share and let Megan have her privacy."

"Okay," he said, having accepted that Sam and Megan were not in a conventional marriage. Despite his urging that it should be.

"When we get to town, I'll be going over to the feed store to pick up ranch supplies. But you take your time at the mercantile to get whatever you need. If you want some material, get that too. I have a good account there and there's money for you to spend on things that please you. And get whatever you need for cooking over the next few weeks. I just bought what was plain and easy to fix, so if there is something that suits you better, feel free to get it."

Gil's horse threw its head back, impatient to move faster than the buggy. "And me and Sam will be glad to eat whatever you want to fix. But I sure wouldn't mind a peach cobbler if you know how."

She laughed, and the delight in her laugh sent a wave of longing through Sam.

"I would love to fix you a cobbler. I'll have fun

picking out things to make for the two of you. I see how hard you work and it's my pleasure to make sure you have a good meal, especially in the evening after being out in that heat all day. But I promise I am a good cook and can make you a hearty meal, complete with dessert."

Sam's stomach growled just thinking about it. She'd already spoiled them, managing to come up with good meals with the supplies he had on hand. What could she do after picking out her own supplies was an exciting thought. God had surely shined on him when that matchmaker matched him up with Megan.

The thought slammed into him like a kick of a mule.

But it was the truth.

CHAPTER SIX

The town was a busy place as they drove up the street. Excitement drummed through Megan so that she could barely contain herself. She'd loved sitting beside Sam and feeling her arm brush his. And he seemed more relaxed than normal and that was very nice.

"That's the hotel. While you're in the store, I'll head over and see about a room before I go to the feed store. I'll be over to fetch you and we'll have a late lunch."

"Okay," she said as he pulled the buggy up to the

front of the store. He hopped from the seat.

Gil had tied the horse and dismounted. He held his hand out to assist Megan from the buggy.

Sam stepped between them. "I'll help my wife step down from the buckboard."

"Sure." Gil chuckled. "I'll see y'all later. I'm going to head on over to Sweet Treats Bakery and get me a treat."

"What about lunch?" Sam asked.

"I'll eat that too," he called without looking back.

Sam shook his head. "That boy loves sweets."

"I can tell."

Megan had taken his hand and he thought he could hold her hand for always. He watched as she grasped her skirt and lifted it out of the way as she climbed down. He almost wished she would trip so he could catch her. Now, that was desperate—for a man to need his wife to trip just so he could have an excuse to hold her. Sam was surely losing his mind.

"Thank you, again, for bringing me. Are you sure there's money for me to buy material?"

"I'm sure. If you want one of those store-bought

dresses they have in there, then get that too."

"I'll look."

"I've seen them hanging up in there. Get one or more if you want them."

"I'll see. But I enjoy making my own dresses. Do you not like them?" Her gaze faltered and he realized in trying to make her happy he might have hurt her feelings.

"Yes, I like them. You look really pretty. I was just wanting you to get what you want."

Relief lit her eyes. "That's very sweet. I'll look."

They stared at each other until she tugged very gently at her hand. Only at the slight tug did he realize she couldn't go anywhere if he kept hanging on to her. He released her hand and felt the rush of heat creep up his neck. "Sorry. I'll be back in an hour and we'll go to the hotel for lunch."

"Okay. See you soon," she said, smiling as she turned and headed into the store.

He smiled too and climbed into the buckboard, grabbed the leathers and watched as she entered the store. He hoped she would be okay on her own. He had a protective streak for her. But Sweet, Texas was about as safe a Texas town as there was. Still, one could never be too careful. He decided he would hurry.

Then again, maybe she needed some time to herself.

~ ~ ~

Megan's stomach was fluttering from the feel of Sam's hand on hers and the look in his eyes. It was as if he didn't want to let her go. She was practically walking on clouds as she entered the store and came face-to-face with a smiling young woman with twinkling eyes. She looked to be a few months pregnant.

"Hello, you must be Sam's wife," the pretty young woman said, her eyes dancing. "I'm Lucy Jones. I'm married to Trey Jones, the sheriff. It's so good to meet you."

"I am Sam's wife, Megan. You're the other mail-order bride." Megan was glad to meet her.

"I am indeed. And I'm so happy to be his wife."

"That's reassuring," Megan said before she could

stop herself. Surely, if she and Gabby were both happy, there was hope for her. "I'm excited to come to town. We're staying at the hotel the next two nights and attending church in the morning."

"Wonderful. That Sam is a good man. I worried about you, though, when I heard that the matchmaker had struck again because you're all the way out there where he lives. Trey said it was a fairly long trip in and you were far more isolated since there wasn't that many neighbors close by. Are you doing okay?"

"I'm adjusting but it is a bit lonesome since he and his brother are working all day. I'm so glad to come to town. I'd love to talk to you and Gabby if there's time before I leave Monday morning."

"I'm glad he brought you in for the service and the church social tomorrow. We will get together and have a talk for certain sometime tomorrow."

She worried suddenly that sounded as if she were unhappy with her husband. She hoped not but she really needed to talk to some other mail-order brides. "That sounds lovely."

"Are you shopping for supplies today? The store

has a great selection."

"I am. And then I'm going to go to the bakery shop and pick up something to bring tomorrow."

"That's so nice but not necessary. We'll have plenty at the potluck."

"I really want to."

"I'm helping out in the store for another hour and then I'm going over to visit with the ladies at the bakery. Let me help you fulfill your list and then we can go over together. And if they're having a slow spot, maybe we can have our chat then."

"I would love that. I thought that you and Gabby would help me navigate this mail-order bride world." She spoke softly so that no one else in this store could hear her.

Lucy smiled and patted her arm. "I can assure you that we do understand."

Feeling relieved, Megan glanced around the store. Her eyes caught on the gingham dress hanging in the back. "That's pretty."

Lucy turned to see what she was looking at. "Come, let me show it to you. It just came in. No one else in town has one like it but looking at you, it could be a little bit big but I'm sure that you know how to sew and could take it in where needed. Then again, we have a lot of pretty material so if you would prefer to make your own, that's available. Or do both."

"That's nice that the store is so well stocked. Sam wanted me to get whatever I need. He's trying to make my life as easy as possible. I thought that was really sweet."

Lucy's smile grew big. "You know, sometimes, before you came along, we would see Sam in town and he just looked so distant. He didn't look that way a few moments ago when he helped you out of the buckboard. I was watching through the window. And he just looked charmed. Sometimes these men out here on the frontier just need a woman's touch."

Megan's skin warmed. "Well, to be honest, that's kind of what I wanted to talk to you all about. I'm just cooking and cleaning for him."

Instead of looking alarmed, Lucy smiled gently. "That's good. When it's right, more will come. It's good that you're giving yourselves time to get to know each other. Now, let's get your order ready and go visit next door at the bakery. You need a flock of women around you."

Megan fingered a piece of lace. "He didn't order me. He didn't want a wife but he decided to marry me anyway. And I decided to marry him but now I fear in doing so, I've given up my hope of ever having children. And I sure would love to hold my own baby in my arms one day."

"I completely understand. I had similar thoughts at one time too. Now, look at me—my little one is going to be here in a few months and I can't wait to hold him or her. Now, let's get your supplies and head over and get you a cherry scone. Everything looks better after one of Ambrosia Mulberry's cherry scones. But wait…Sam may have plans for you two to eat lunch together. If so, then we can go afterwards."

"I am supposed to eat lunch with him." Megan wanted to have lunch with Sam but also wanted to spend time with the ladies. She wasn't sure a scone could fix her troubles but some social time with other women would help.

Lucy pulled the dress from the hanger and smiled. "Great. The way Sam was smiling at you when he dropped you off wasn't like you were the cleaning lady. It was like a man looking forward to spending time with you. We'll go to the bakery after you have lunch, if that works for you."

Megan's heart lifted. *Could it be true? Could she and Sam actually be on the road to something more?* She almost hated to hope.

~ ~ ~

Sam walked into the feed store wishing he was with Megan at the store. It was just his luck that there was a crowd of old fellas hanging out when he entered.

"Well, look who come to town," Chauncey Todd said, a wide tobacco-stained grin on his face. "You bring your new bride to town with ya?"

Horace Holcomb scratched his chin and glared at his old buddy. "I just told you I saw her riding beside him when he drove into town. Can't you hear?"

Chauncey chuckled. "Yeah, I just wanted to tease

him a bit."

Sam figured he was going to get a lot of teasing from the old-timers.

Big John came out of the back. "You boys leave Sam alone. How's it going, Sam?"

"It's going pretty good. I have a list for you."

"Well, that's mighty nice. You hand that to me and I'll get that brought together, and you can pick it up in your buckboard here in just a little while. Or if you want, go back to the hotel—you know we'll load it for you. If you brought that pretty bride of yours to town, I'm sure you want to go over there and have a good meal at the hotel."

How did Big John know something like that? The man grinned as if he read his mind.

"Well, thank you, Big John. That's exactly what I was thinking about doing. Megan has been cooking for me and Gil all week and I figured that she needed a nice meal cooked for her and since I'm a terrible cook, the hotel was the best choice." That made everyone laugh.

Chauncey and Horace cackled like hyenas.

"That is so romantic," Horace said. "I tell you what—I just don't know what to think about all these pretty little women coming to town and turning you young bucks into romantic knots." He scratched his head as if in confusion.

Chauncey chuckled. "It don't hurt nothing for them to want to have a little sweetness in their lives. It brings out the best in a man. I don't talk about it much but I had me a sweetheart of a wife a long time ago. She died and broke my heart. I don't talk about it anymore. But Sam, I'm real happy for you. It's lonesome out there where we live. I get lonesome but it suits me and my old mule but it ain't healthy for a guy like you. Or for Gil, either. I think it's wonderful what this matchmaker did bringing her here for you."

Everybody had gone quiet, looking at Chauncey. For a man who never said much of anything, he'd just said a whole lot. And nobody had known that he had lost a wife. They knew that Mr. Sweet had lost his wife and Big John lost his Millie. But nobody knew Chauncey had ever even had a soft enough side to him that a woman would get within ten feet of him.

Sam smiled kindly at the old miner, only now learning of his heartache. "Thank you, Chauncey. And I'm very sorry for your loss. I know it was a long time ago but I'm still so sorry."

"I am too," John added, cupping the miner's shoulder in a heartfelt grip. "I know it was hard on me when I lost Millie. And I know what you're saying, about the sweeter side of life. That's what a woman is for a man. A woman softens up us ornery old men— and young men too."

"Yep, that'd be true." Chauncey grinned.

Horace chuckled. "I guess we know what Big John thinks of us."

Chauncey spat tobacco into the spittoon, making a bull's-eye right into the opening. "Can't deny what's true."

Sam figured Chauncey and Horace were not as rough as they pretended to be. He also knew they enjoyed cupcakes made by Mrs. Ambrosia and were at any gathering they were the sweets being served. He also knew they didn't spend all their money at the saloon down the street. They'd rather spend their time here, huddled up with Big John and harassing his customers instead of getting drunk and wasting their money gambling. Sam respected them for that.

Before Megan had been brought here by the stagecoach and some mystery matchmaker to marry him, he'd been pretty sour himself and pretty grumpy. And he understood it now, because he hadn't had anything to look forward to at the end of the day. He'd just worked. And so had Gil.

"Truth is, fellows, I don't know who brought Megan into my life by lying to her and pretending to be me, but I was mad about that at first. But I couldn't turn her back after she'd come so far. Now the ranch is a whole lot nicer. And as crazy as it sounds, if I were to ever find out who that person is who lied about being me and wrote that letter, I'd probably give him or her a hug."

There, he'd been honest.

"I'll tell you what," Big John said. "I figure that it won't take long for this matchmaker to know you're a happy man. It's written all over your face. You be nice to that sweet girl and things will just get better. You need some little kids running around now."

Sam swallowed hard. *Kids.* Yeah, he wanted kids but he was trying to get his marriage figured out. He wondered whether... He cringed suddenly, remembering the day Megan had said she would like more from the marriage. Had she only agreed to everything he said he wanted, like being his cook, that they'd sleep in separate rooms and she'd given up on what she wanted?

What had he done? Could he fix this? He needed to go find the preacher. He needed to talk; he needed to find out if what he was thinking was wrong or right. And he needed to do it fast.

CHAPTER SEVEN

After she'd given the list she'd written down to Lucy and they'd gathered the supplies together, feeling a bit frivolous, she'd added the pretty dress to the supplies and enough material for her to make herself two more dresses.

When she spotted Sam coming across the road toward the store, her heart raced at the sight of him and she sighed.

"I heard that," Lucy said.

Megan looked at her in shock, not having realized her sigh had been audible.

Lucy looked mischievously at her. "It's okay. You should like looking at your husband. And he looks determined. You know, everything between me and Trey wasn't perfect at first either. He hired me to watch Janie. I was just here to take care of his little girl. But things changed when we started caring for each other. I'm confident from what I'm seeing that things will work out for you too."

"I do hope you're right." She sighed again, unable to hide what her heart had come to desire as Sam entered the store.

He swept his hat from his head and held it over his heart. "Did you get what you wanted?"

She noticed he didn't say needed, but wanted. The word choice sent a nice feeling through her.

She thought of what her stepfather had waiting for her back home and cringed inwardly. She was blessed and she knew it. "I did. Lucy helped me."

"Great. I thought we could go to the hotel for lunch."

Megan looked at Lucy, not sure what to say.

"Great choice," Lucy said. "I'm so glad you

brought Megan into town. You finish eating and if you have any more errands to run, please bring Megan by the house and we'll walk over to the sweet shop and see Gabby and the ladies. We'd all enjoy visiting with her."

Megan smiled in relief and appreciation at Lucy. "If that works out for you, then I would love that."

"I'm sure you would enjoy visiting with all the ladies so I could do some more errands. I thought I'd visit with Trey a little too."

"Perfect. He took the morning off today so he and Janie could work on the playhouse he's building in the backyard. They're having some father-daughter time but I'm sure he'd love to see you."

Sam's brows crinkled over serious eyes. "I wouldn't want to intrude."

"By the time you get there, he'll be heading back over to the sheriff's office and you can visit there. Janie will go with us to the bakery. She adores the bakery."

"Then that works well." He looked at Megan. "Now it's time for me to treat you to a meal you don't have to prepare. If you'll excuse us, we'll see you soon."

"You'll love the food over there. It's really delicious."

Megan took the arm he offered her, feeling a little embarrassed but so happy to see Sam. She had the most pleasant hum going on inside her from the feel of his hand at the base of her back as he led her from the store.

Moments later, they were walking down the sidewalk and she felt so proud to be walking beside him. He was so handsome. She wasn't sure what the future held for them but right now she just wanted to enjoy the moment. And to trust that things were going to be fine. She was going to enjoy being in town with him, having lunch with him at the hotel, and then going to church with him tomorrow.

A few minutes later, they took their seats in the nearly empty dining room. It was a little bit later than normal lunch hours so she suspected if there was a lunch crowd, it had cleared out. She wondered where Gil was but she figured he was old enough to get his own meal so she didn't ask about him. Truth be known, she was going to enjoy having a meal with just her husband. Sam had held her chair for her as she sat down, startling her and making her feel special.

He took the menu from the hostess and held it out to her. "Order what you like."

Their hands brushed as she took the menu from him. Butterflies fluttered again in her chest. "It all looks good." Her voice sounded breathless.

"It is." His eyes were warm as he watched her.

She focused on the menu. She could smell the delicious scents coming from the kitchen.

"Are you ready to order?" the waitress asked. "The dish of the day is chicken and dressing."

"That sounds wonderful. I'll have that, please." She smiled at the waitress.

"A very good choice. Our cook makes a wonderful dressing and chicken and dumplings, too. I'll have him put a dumpling on the plate too."

Sam ordered a steak with the side dressing. After the waitress had gone, he took a sip of his water. "So did you get you some material and maybe a dress?"

"I did. I got one dress—it was so pretty—and then I got material for two. I might have to take the dress that was already made up a little bit but not much."

"Can you sew a dress?"

"Yes, I sew quite well, and not just table cloths."

"I have a feeling you can do whatever you set your mind to quite well."

"Thank you." She blushed at the compliment.

They sat there awkwardly for a few moments and she wondered whether this was how it would be always. She hoped they could get comfortable with each other. If they could become at ease with each other, that would be so lovely.

"I was able to get our rooms."

"That's good. We won't have to sleep in the stable," she said, teasing him.

He chuckled. "No, no stable for us. I've already taken our bags up." He stared at her. "Did I tell you how pretty you look today?"

His words startled her, they were so unexpected. She brought her hand up, smoothed her hair and pushed the wayward strand behind her ear. "No, but thank you."

"You're welcome."

Their food came and they ate as he talked about how he wanted to build the ranch up and build the stock up and maybe one day add onto the house. She wondered whether he had thoughts of children in that bigger house or maybe that building the ranch up was because he wanted children to leave it to. She could see them running around and playing with their daddy. Thinking about it, her heart ached with longing. Sam was such a good man. She really hoped more and more that there was room in his heart for her. Room in his heart for children.

~ ~ ~

After lunch, Sam held his arm out so that his wife could slip her hand into the crook of his arm as he walked her down the sidewalk toward Trey and Lucy Jones's home. It was just off the main drive and a short but pleasant walk. He was enjoying her company and was becoming more and more familiar with the constant buzz of awareness that he felt at the soft touch of her hand, like now with it resting in his elbow.

"It's a nice day for a walk," he said, feeling himself relax as they strolled together. *When was the last time he'd relaxed?*

"It is. And it's been nice spending time with you."

Her quiet words had his steps slowing. "I feel the same way. But, working the ranch is a lot of work. I only have so many hours in the day to get the work done and even though Gil is there, building a herd and building the fence to keep them in just takes long hours."

"I know. I didn't mean to complain. I just meant that this all means a lot to me."

He halted and turned to her. Unable to stop his hand, that suddenly had a mind of its own, he cupped her jaw. His fingertips brushed her soft neck and he felt her swallow hard, as if nervous. Her luminous blue eyes widened. "You are a surprise to me," he said, feeling emotions he wasn't sure what to do with.

"Is that a good thing?" She looked worried.

"Yes." He chuckled. "Very good."

Her mouth had fallen open. "You laughed." Her sudden smile was brilliant. "You should do that more often."

His brows bunched over narrowed eyes. "You're right. I do need to do it more." His thumb rubbed back and forth against her skin. "With you around, I believe that won't be a problem," he murmured and then gently kissed her parted lips. He felt her intake of breath and pulled back, realizing they were standing on the open street just off the square.

Her eyes twinkled then filled with tears. "That makes me happy."

"Then, don't cry," he said, panicked by the threat of tears.

She sniffed and her smile widened. "I'm not. I mean, I'm sorry. It's yesterday and then today, I just wasn't expecting to come to town and then we've come here and you're saying things I wasn't expecting. I'm just a little overwhelmed."

"Well, don't be. Just relax. Let's get going

because Lucy is waiting on you and then you're going to go see the new sweet shop and have some more of that female time."

He started walking and she fell into step with him. They turned the corner and saw Lucy sitting on the front porch. She had her hand resting on her swollen stomach as if protecting her unborn child. Janie, the little girl, was running in the yard with a stick she held up in the air as a ribbon trailed out behind it in the air.

He stopped at the fence as a sudden picture filled his mind of Megan sitting on their porch, holding his child and their older child playing in the yard. His knees got a little weak.

"Hello," Lucy called and Janie spun to see them.

"Are you okay?" Megan asked him.

"I'm fine. Just fine." He opened the low picket fence gate and let her walk through. "Hi, Lucy. Hello, Janie."

"Hello," Lucy called. "Trey said to meet him at the office."

"I'll do that. You ladies have a good afternoon. I'll

see you back at the hotel later."

"Okay," Megan said, her eyes still wide as she looked at him.

He had the urge to take her in his arms but that was not appropriate with the little girl watching. He turned and walked away.

He needed to talk to Trey. To Jarred. He needed advice.

CHAPTER EIGHT

Trey was in the office when Sam walked in.

"I heard you were in town. How are you doing?"

Sam frowned. "Not good. How did you do it? I'm in a fix."

Trey laughed, leaned back in his chair and studied him. "Let me guess, you're talking about your new wife?"

"Yes. I'm a rancher. I work. I'm set in my ways and suddenly I'm feeling all out of sorts." He started pacing as everything that was bottled up inside him boiled up.

"I know that feeling. Happened to me."

"Really? I mean, I'm feeling things I never felt before. Like when she tears up, it slams me in the chest like a bull kicked me. And I'm seeing babies in my mind. And all I can think of is holding her in my arms and…well, it's not right for me to talk about what I'm feeling. I don't know what to do."

He stopped pacing and sank into the chair across the desk from Trey, who looked at him with understanding.

"You haven't…you know, made the marriage a marriage?"

"No. I just don't feel right. I feel like she deserves a husband who loves her."

"And that means you don't want to be her husband anymore?"

"No, I just worry that I won't be what she wants."

"But you're seeing babies, so does that mean you're falling for her?"

"I, I…" He paused. "Yes."

"Then why are you worried? You're who she married. She came here to marry you."

"She came here to marry the man who wrote to her in my name."

"But she married you. Don't forget that. Lucy and I had a rough start. That matchmaker is really good at surprising people. I won't lie—we were overwhelmed at first. But we found our way and I think you will too."

Sam hated to admit it, but fear pricked at him and he decided to just come right out and say it. "What if I try to make this work and then Megan realizes she made a mistake coming out here?"

Trey looked at him in dismay. "You are falling for her and you're going to keep it to yourself?"

"No. I mean, yes, I'm falling for her. And no, I'm not going to keep it to myself. I have reservations— what if she ends up hating living all the way out at my place? She's been there for a week and she got all teary-eyed and wanted to come to town. She couldn't stand being out there that long. And it was her first week."

"She'll adjust. And you'll teach her to drive the buggy so she could make the trip into town on her own if she needs to."

"I don't know about that. It's a long trip for her to be making on her own."

"That's something you and she will have to work out, but you'll adjust. Like you coming to town for church and the picnic tomorrow. That'll help her."

"Maybe so."

"You getting comfortable with having her out there and the feelings you're feeling will help."

He thought about that. Maybe if he gave in to the need to hold her, it would help her to feel like she wasn't so alone out there. The idea struck him and instantly his entire body warmed to the idea. "I'll try to do that."

"Try? I wouldn't think it would be a hard thing to do. But for a man like you, one who keeps to himself, I'm sure that would be harder to do."

"But the more I think about it, the more I realize that I married her and that means I have a responsibility to her needs too."

Trey smiled. "I think you're catching on. That means you got to think about her and not just yourself.

You've got to step out of your comfort zone. Jarred helped me realize this."

Sam knew that Trey and Pastor Andrews were good friends, so him calling the pastor by his first name seemed natural. "I need to talk to him too."

"Might be a good idea."

~ ~ ~

The sweet shop was nice. It was white washed and had counters with glass cases so you could see all the food. The instant Megan walked inside with Lucy and little Janie, the place broke out in excited squeals.

"Oh, look who is here," Mrs. Mulberry exclaimed, clapping her hands together and hustling from behind the counter. "We are so happy you came to see us. Essie Jane, come see who Lucy brought to see us."

"We are really glad you came to town." Gabby came around to hug her. "And you and Sam are doing well?" she asked, encouragingly.

Before she could answer, a woman gasped. "Oh, my oh my." The tiny, thin woman hustled from the kitchen area. She had on an apron and was wiping her hands on it as she hurried toward Megan. "We have been discussing you." She threw her frail arms around Megan and gave a gentle hug. "Are you doing okay way out there?"

Taken by surprise, Megan was touched. "It is so good to see all of you. I'm overwhelmed by your sweet greetings."

"Oh, they are sincere, I can assure you," Mrs. Mulberry said.

"We brought her here to get a cake." Janie smiled back at them from where she stared at the sweets on the other side of the glass. "Can I have one too, Mama?"

"Yes, you can," Lucy said. "Pick out what you want and Gabby will get it for you. You can eat it and play with the dollhouse while we visit. How does that sound?"

"Good. I love Mrs. Mulberry's dollhouse."

Mrs. Mulberry beamed proudly at Megan. "Placing that dollhouse in here for the little ones to play with was one of my better ideas," she told everyone.

"This bakery was one of your better ideas too," Gabby said. "It gave me a job and sure has made a lot of people happy."

"Me too," Essie Jane said. "It gave me something other than quilting to do. And we even hold our quilting meetings here sometimes. Nothing better than quilting and eating good pastries. You'll have to come to town and join us sometimes."

Feeling happy and speechless at the same time from their warm embraces, both physically and socially, she searched for words. "I hope to do that. It's just so far. And Sam works all the time, so I'd have to come into town by myself. I'm not sure I can do that."

"Sit down, and I'll bring out coffee and a platter of pastries and we'll figure this out," Mrs. Mulberry said. "You will get used to the country out here. Coming from the city, it does feel a little overwhelming but with a buggy and a good horse, you can do it. Or we could come out to see you."

The fact that the older woman seemed so confident about what she could do gave her a little courage. Really, why had she suddenly gotten fearful? She'd ridden a stagecoach all the way out here by herself—she could ride a few hours in a buggy.

Everyone sat around a bench table and Ambrosia, as she was told to call Mrs. Mulberry, and Essie Jane had food and coffee set out in moments. Janie was humming from the corner where she sat with her back to them as she played with an adorable dollhouse. It was all so comforting.

She took a delectable cherry scone from the plate and waited as everyone took a pastry. She added cream and sugar to her coffee and then sipped it. "I needed this." She had the best feeling about this group of women. "Thank you."

"Me too," Lucy said. "Janie and I bake but it just tastes better when someone else bakes it." She sighed as she took a bite of a peach pastry. "Ladies, this is fantastic."

"That's Ambrosia's recipe," Essie Jane said. "She has always had a way with pastry. Megan, what do you think about that scone? They cannot be beaten. And your Sam loves them."

"So does my Jarred." Gabby smiled as Megan bit into the scone.

"Oh my goodness," she muttered over the bite that sent cherry flavor bursting through her taste buds. "Delicious."

"Yes, they are." Lucy laughed. "Trey loves them, too. Face it, Ambrosia knew the way to our husbands' hearts before we did. They love her."

"And I love them. That's one reason I had the idea for the bakery. There are just so many single men out here on this Texas frontier who need a little sweetness in their lives. I love having a place they can come when they are in town and pick up a pastry or a whole cake or pie if they want it."

"I'll have to learn or take some home with me. We put some things on the supply list that will enable me to bake them some sweets. Sam and Gil haven't had many, other than what they get from you when they come to town. Those men live off beans, bacon, and jerky, I think."

Ambrosia looked slyly at her. "Whoever the matchmaker is knew men in need were those two. And you're a good one to rescue them."

It crossed her mind that the matchmaker could be Mrs. Ambrosia Mulberry. The thought must have been clearly in her eyes.

"No, it's not me," the sweet lady declared. "Many people have thought that but I can assure you it is not me. But I'm willing to help whoever it is out as much as I can. I love the idea of all of you wonderful, brave women coming out here. And so far, whoever our matchmaker is, they have picked very deserving men as the grooms. I'm very pleased about that and trying to figure out who the next one will be, if there is one. That Deputy Donavan could sure use someone. That poor fellow can't cook a lick and he lives in a tiny house on the outskirts of town that is about as colorless as they come."

"I think he would fall over if a bride showed up for him," Lucy said. "But it would be nice. He's so helpful to Trey and this entire town."

She was happy to know that everyone thought so much of Sam. He was a good man and she had known it from early on. She felt proud to be his wife in that moment. She hadn't met the deputy but they talked good about him, too. "I feel blessed to be here. And I'm going to get used to it. I would be overjoyed if his ranch had been a little closer."

"You know," Gabby's eyes twinkled. "Jarred and I are planning on building a few miles out on the way to your place. So that would get us an hour closer to you. And there are a couple of cowboys out that way who are also single. Maybe the matchmaker will hear your wish and fix those two fellas up. And you'll have neighbors."

The thought excited her. "That would be wonderful. The more women who come out here, the better it will be."

Essie Jane beamed brightly. "And you know, there is always Gil. That boy is a man now too."

"That's true." Megan chuckled. "I might send off for a wife for him. He is twenty. He just seems so much younger than Sam."

"Sam's always had the most responsibility and that adds to a man's age." Ambrosia sipped her coffee. "That's why I was so happy to see you arrive in town. I haven't seen him yet but someone came in here earlier and said he sure seemed happier."

"I agree," Lucy said. "When he came into the store earlier, he had eyes only for you. And then when he was walking you to my house, you two looked so happy. Are you happy?"

Megan inhaled and let her insides calm as they'd started churning. "I'm a little scared." She leaned forward and whispered, "Right now, I'm really only the cook."

All but Lucy went slack-jawed.

"You aren't…" Ambrosia said, without finishing her words.

"That is correct," Megan said, softly. "At this rate, I'll never have the family I long for. And I don't know how to fix it. He did kiss me yesterday for the second time since the wedding." She didn't say anything about his touch earlier that was so endearing and confusing.

"That's a good sign," Lucy said. "I think he's just adjusting to the situation. Remember, he was surprised by your arrival. You were prepared. I think that's the thing to remember."

"True," Ambrosia practically cooed.

And Essie Jane agreed with a hearty nod of her head. "So very true. You just have to keep making him glad you're in his life."

It was true. He'd agreed to marry her but maybe he was just adjusting. Maybe the kiss and his bringing her to town were signs that he was adjusting to having a wife. And the more she could do to make him glad she was in his life, the better.

"Thank you all. I knew I needed some female support to help me understand. I'm going to be the best wife he could ever want and pray he falls in love with me."

"Everything will work out," Gabby assured her.

She prayed it would; though skeptical, she would do everything in her power to help it be so.

CHAPTER NINE

He was on his to find the pastor when him walking down the sidewalk.

"Hi, Sam," Jarred called as soon as he spotted Sam. "I'm glad you're in town. I was thinking about bringing Gabby out to see your new bride one day next week, but here you are. You did bring Megan to town, too, I'm assuming?"

"I did. She needs some time to adjust to being all the way out there at the ranch. And she asked to come to church also. We needed supplies, so I figured it was a good time to come into town."

"Good. I know that took time away from your work; however, I'm pleased you realize your wife has needs too."

"I'm learning. I was just talking to Trey and before that I was over at the feed store and all the old men were saying I needed to think about her. And I am. But to be honest, I'm not sure what all I need to be doing. I was hoping to talk to you and Trey, since you two have been through this."

Jarred grinned. "Court her. I had to do it and so did Trey. It helps. And yes, you are already married but you still need special time to get to know each other. And since you'll be at the church social tomorrow, it will be a perfect day for fun and enjoying yourselves without work interfering. There will be festivities. You two participate and have fun. It will be good for both of you. It will help the two of you figure your own way."

When he left soon after, Sam's mind was full. He didn't know how to court a woman. He'd been working and building up the ranch but he figured if he set his mind to it, he could learn to court Megan. When he reached the hotel, he waited in the lobby for Megan.

Gil came in from the dining room and found him there. He was grinning. "I just had me a real good steak." He rubbed his stomach.

"Why didn't you wait on me and Megan for supper?"

"You get to eat with me every evening. I figured you two could use some meals alone. Where is Megan?"

So his little brother did have his head on straight. "Thanks for thinking of us. She's at the sweet shop, visiting with a bunch of the women. What have you been doing today?"

"I went over to the livery and talked to Levi. He's just bought a new stud horse. He's going to start breeding it soon and I'm thinking about getting me a horse for an investment."

"Really? How long have you been thinking about that?" Sam asked, surprised at hearing this from Gil, more evidence that his little brother was maturing. Levi was about his same age and they had been friends since Levi had come to town a couple of years ago.

"Not long. But, you getting a pretty wife has got me to thinking about what I have to offer a wife."

"You have the same as me to offer one. Are you thinking about a wife too?"

"Well, not exactly at this moment. But Megan is a great gal and I can't help but think about having a good woman waiting for me in the evenings."

"Okay, that's good." He didn't say more because he was having his own situation to figure out. "Breeding horses is smart thinking. I'm impressed. I like it."

"You do?" Gil grinned and stood a little straighter. "I was kind of afraid to mention it."

"Why?"

"Because you always have everything figured out and I just do what you tell me."

Sam suddenly felt hard hit. "It's your ranch, too. You have a say in it, Gil. If you have ideas, then I want to hear them."

"Okay," he said, just as Megan walked into the hotel.

She looked relaxed and had a basket with a

colorful cloth over it. She held the basket up. "I brought a cake for the picnic potluck tomorrow."

She smiled and it slammed Sam in the gut. She was beautiful and he liked the happiness shining in her eyes. *Was this how she would look if she lived closer to town?* He'd never thought about how far out his ranch was. He'd always been fine for the most part but now he wished it was closer. For her sake, because he wanted that look on her face as much as possible.

"What kind is it?" Gil went over and lifted the cloth. "That smells so good, like cinnamon. Can I have a piece?"

She laughed. "Yes, it's cinnamon and no, you cannot. It's for tomorrow."

"Well, it didn't hurt to ask. I'm going up to my room and give you two some time to yourselves." He grinned. "This place is really nice. I'm looking forward to sleeping in that nice fluffy bed."

"Well, don't get too comfortable." Sam lowered his voice. "I'll be in to take up half of it after I get Megan settled in for the night."

Gil scowled and hissed, "She's your wife. Share a

bed with her."

Sam wanted to more than he could express, but it just wouldn't be right. *Would it?* He waited until Gil was out of earshot before he looked at his wife. She was blushing.

"You could stay in the room with me." She leaned in closer to him so that no one could hear what she said.

He didn't say anything as he stared into her eyes, wanting more than she could know to take her up on that offer. Instead, he took the basket from her hand and led her back to the dining room for supper. He listened as she told of her afternoon with the ladies and how much she enjoyed them. He enjoyed just sitting across from her and watching her happiness. She needed more of this. More companionship. But how was he supposed to make that happen? Matt Silver was his closest neighbor and he worked as hard as Sam and Gil. Sam wasn't sure how he felt about a wife but if the man got one, that would mean a closer neighbor for Megan.

Sam wondered whether the mystery matchmaker

took requests.

The thought made his lip twitch upward. He'd come a long way from the day he'd received the letter that he'd have a mail-order bride waiting for him at the stagecoach.

~ ~ ~

When they'd finished dinner, he crooked his arm and Megan slipped hers through his and they walked toward the stairs. He carried the basket with the cake in one hand as they walked up the stairs. His pulse raced faster with each step. Every step, he debated what he should do. He was really feeling like the temperature in the room had gone up really high the closer he got to the second floor and the rooms that he had rented. It seemed hotter than a Texas July during a drought by the time they'd reached her door. He hoped he wasn't sweating bullets, but his forehead sure felt damp.

Part of his debate with himself was that if he stayed in the room with his brother and then people in town found out, they might think things between him and Megan weren't good. *Would they think him and his new bride were having a fight? Would they think he didn't find his new bride attractive? How would his staying with Gil make Megan feel?*

That question stopped him short. It was the first time he'd thought of her side of this debate. She'd offered for him to stay. There was a big bed. He could sleep on one side and she the other. When he carried the cake into the room and closed the door behind him, he saw the couch too. He'd forgotten about the couch. And then he noticed his bag sat on the floor next to hers.

She turned to look at him, uncertainty churning in her beautiful eyes. He swallowed hard.

"I don't mind you sleeping in the same room with me. You are my husband."

She had a point, but he didn't trust himself. "I'll just get my things out and go in there with Gil for the night."

He saw hurt in her eyes. His heart thundered something fierce. She was his bride. They'd been married for over a week.

But he wanted to court her.

He was trying to do right by her. But there *had* been hurt in her eyes.

"Please wait." She halted him. He turned back to her. "I know I'm not what you were looking for. And I know you didn't want me here. But I promise you I'll try to be the wife that you want me to be. I talked with Gabby and Lucy today. I didn't tell them everything, but I told them that our marriage wasn't real, so far. That I was just the maid. But I confessed that I want children and I fear I'll never have them."

He had thought she might talk to them like he'd talked to Trey and Jarred but, still, realizing that these ladies now knew their private business bothered him. But he'd done it, too, so it wasn't right him to feel a nagging irritation over it. Then again, if he'd given her more space to tell him her feelings, maybe she wouldn't have had to talk to the ladies. "I see. And what did they say?"

"They told me I needed to be completly honest with you. So I'm being honest. I would love to have a baby of my own. And if you sleep in another room forever, that will never happen. Do you not find me attractive?" Her gaze dropped to the floor as his stomach did too.

She thought she didn't appeal to him. That he didn't want her.

He strode back to her and before she could say anything more, he took her in his arms and, driven by her confession, he took her lips with his. She hesitated then melted into him, responding to his kiss like she had yesterday. He pulled her closer, lost in the moment.

He couldn't think straight, could only think about how wonderful kissing her was. "I want you. I was just wanting to give you time to adjust."

"I'm adjusted," she breathed against his lips.

And that was all he needed to make his mind up about the night. "Are you sure about this?" he whispered, looking into her eyes.

She nodded and in the next moment, he scooped her into his arms and carried her to the bed.

CHAPTER TEN

The next morning, Sam felt as if he could climb the highest peak. He hadn't known how beautiful it would be being with his bride.

His bride.

Holding her in his arms when he woke had been an amazing feeling. It had instantly made him aware of how alone he'd been before she came into his life. After they'd dressed, he pulled her into his arms and held her. "Thank you for last night. I'm glad you're here."

She smiled and it sent a spark to his heart. He was

coming to care for her.

"Thank you. I didn't know what to expect but…it was more than I imagined."

That made him happy. "Good. Now, let's go have breakfast and then we'll go to church and then this picnic you've been looking forward to."

"That sounds wonderful. It's going to be a lovely day. I'm so glad we came. Thank you."

Her thanking him seemed wrong and he placed a finger to her pretty, perfect lips. "No more thank-yous, okay? I should have offered earlier to bring you to town. I shouldn't have let you think all week that I wasn't interested in you, in us. I do have work, but I will try to meet your needs as often as I can from here on out. You just might have to give me a nudge sometimes and let me know what you need. I'm new at this husband duty."

She smiled and squeezed him around the waist. "I'll try to be a good wife too. I'm new also."

He kissed her smiling lips and wanted to skip church and the picnic and spend the day with her here in this room, just the two of them. But that wouldn't be right. So he released her and then headed to the door. It was time to reenter the world.

~ ~ ~

Megan was floating as she and her husband left the room. Their night together had been so wonderful. Just thinking about it made her skin warm with pleasure. The first person they saw on the way down the stairs was Gil.

He hitched a brow at his brother. "Glad you decided to stay in your room. I enjoyed that big bed all to myself."

She blushed as Sam gave his little brother an easy shove to the shoulder. "I would much rather share a soft bed with my bride than the likes of you."

Gil grinned and her cheeks heated more but she was pleased by Sam's words. Her world was coming into a wonderful place and she felt warm and amazing. God was good.

They had breakfast in the restaurant and then went to church. Pastor Andrews did a wonderful job of preaching about how God built the church to encourage people to come together for fellowship. At his words, Megan was heartened when Sam gently squeezed her hand that he'd been holding all through the service. She felt as if the service had been preached just to them, to remind them that coming to town to have fellowship with others was a good thing. She really felt in her heart that her life was balancing out now. That she could have the life here she'd been dreaming of ever since she ran away from the horrible man who would have ruined her. She was ever more thankful for the ad that had changed her life. And she knew she was forever grateful for the matchmaker who'd placed the ad.

~ ~ ~

After church, the picnic was fine. They spread a blanket out on the ground and Sam helped her sit down on the blanket. He held her hand as she fixed her skirts beneath her and then he sat down beside her with full plates from the potluck spread that everyone had contributed to. Gil, again, hung out with the single men; there were several. Far less married people than single males. She had noticed this in church, too, and she assumed that for every single male in church, there was probably more not attending. She realized how hard it was to get to town from all the surrounding areas and it hit her anew why the matchmaker was doing this. She and the ladies had discussed it yesterday too. Sweet, Texas was on the verge of dying if no women and children were here to help it survive.

"This fried chicken is wonderful," she said. "Since I now have supplies, I'll be able to cook a wider range of dishes for you. But we'd need to raise chickens for me to give you fried chicken."

Sam took a bite of a chicken leg and nodded. When he was finished chewing, he spoke up. "We could raise chickens if you're up for it."

"Yes. And fresh eggs would be good, too."

"Then we'll do it. I'm interested in tasting some of your chicken. You're a very good cook. I can tell from just what you've cooked with the limited supplies that I had when you came that you could do great things with the right supplies."

"Thank you. I don't think you'll hate me or anything."

He laughed and it caused that warm, happy feeling to course through her. "I don't think we have any worry about that. I could never hate you. I don't know if you've noticed, but I'm falling for you, Mrs. McKay."

Her heart caught, sending a sharp ache through her. *Could it be true?* She hadn't been sure whether their beautiful night together had been more than him just wanting to be with her or whether his heart was beginning to open to her as hers was to him. She was not used to having her heart involved; she had never been in love or truly courted by a suitor, so this was all new to her. She'd hoped, but until now she hadn't known whether he was beginning to truly care for her.

"That makes me so happy." She felt as if her world was finally starting to look like the life she'd always dreamed of, a loving husband and babies in her future. And friends. She just needed time with her husband and surely he would fall as madly in love with her as she was falling in love with him.

~ ~ ~

Big John studied the crowd at the church social. He had several cowboys on his list and had sent out a few letters. Things looked as if they were moving along nicely for Megan and Sam. He was glad. It was always a relief when the bride came to town and then they went ahead and married, because at least part of the battle was won right then.

However, he knew there was a problem with how far Sam lived from town, being all the way on the outskirts of the county. Why the man's parents had settled land so far away from everyone else was a mystery to Big John. But they'd settled a big spread using all of their names and one day, Big John had no doubt that Sam and Gil would have one of the best ranches in all of Texas. They were smart and hard-working and that was one of the reasons Big John had meddled in Sam's life. That and the fact that the man just seemed lonesome.

But being that far away was really hard on a female. And he needed to help with that situation. After all, he was responsible for putting Megan out there.

Big John's gaze rested on Matt Silver. Matt's ranch was next in line from Sam and Gil's, which was only about two hours ride from town. That was much better than the half a day ride out to Sam's place. A wife might do Matt some good, like it seemed Sam's new wife was for him. Then there was Gil, an obvious choice to marry off and give Megan another female out there in the country. But Gil seemed almost too young to marry. He hadn't yet proved to John that he was truly looking toward his future. That worried John, that Gil wasn't quite ready yet.

Still, he had letters out for both him and Matt. He never had two mail-order brides come to town at the same time for two grooms, and he'd taken a chance on this when he'd sent letters out for Gil and Matt. Gil's letter had been simply on a gut instinct and now John was worried that he should have not listened to his gut. But his intuition told him not to worry.

He hoped his intuition was right as it usually was. *And wasn't he something*, he thought, thinking of Millie, *me, sounding like I'm a wheeler and a dealer on this matchmaking*. He wasn't; with only three matches under his belt, he better not get cocky. He was blessed that he hadn't been found out yet. He needed to focus and make sure it stayed that way because he was just getting started with matching these young bucks up. Yes, he still struggled with a bit of guilt at what he was doing behind everyone's backs. But, at the end of the day, to see his smiling matches and see the love they shared…well, that did his old heart good. And after losing his Millie, he needed something to help his heart rekindle some life that Millie's passing had taken from him.

So, he would continue to be the mystery matchmaker of Sweet, Texas.

And he would carry that title proudly, although secretly.

After all, who would ever suspect him, a giant of a man?

They'd suspected the women's quilting club—it

made sense, after all. Speculation had them as the most suspected group—but he'd begun to think people had decided the ladies were telling the truth because *all* of the women denied it and were now the ones watching for clues of who the matchmaker might be.

However, Ambrosia Mulberry and Essie Jane seemed undeniably happy that the brides were coming to town. And they had, in some ways, helped him help the marriages succeed. Both with Lucy and Trey and then with Pastor Jarred and Gabby, they'd encouraged the brides along the way. And after seeing Lucy and Megan at the bakery earlier the day before, he thought maybe they were helping out some more. And the bakery was the perfect gathering spot for all the ladies in town to gather for tea, sweets, and encouragement…or gossip. The men visited and ate the delicious treats but they didn't linger. In more ways than one, the bakery had been a miracle. And a blessing.

Gil and Levi, the livery stable owner, were having a big conversation and well, his mind was preoccupied with Matt Silver. Big John couldn't help moving over to see whether he could find out what they were discussing. Levi was another one John had his eyes on. He was about the same age as Gil, around twenty. He owned his own business and was a hard worker; however, Levi still lived in a little apartment at the back of the livery stable and that was no place for a bride. Still, he was an enterprising young man and Big John figured he was one to watch.

And, unable to stop himself from thinking he might need a bride to help him along with his plans, he'd sent out a letter on Levi's behalf.

"How's it going Gil? Levi?" he asked as he came close to the young men. They both looked at him. Gil gave his usual easy grin. Levi gave him a nod and a thoughtful stare, and Big John could almost see his mind working.

"Big John, you might be just the man we need to talk to," Levi said. "I have bought myself a new stallion—you might've seen me bring him into town."

"I did see a fine-looking horse with you the other day. Are you going to start breeding?"

Levi looked proud. "Yes, sir, I am. My only

problem is I don't know if I can manage it at the livery. It doesn't need a high-spirited stallion disturbing all the other horses boarding there. So I've had my eye on a small piece of land out from town on the way toward Gil and Sam's ranch. Gil is going to be my first customer. He's buying him a mare and going to go into the horse business. This little piece of land between his ranch and town has Matt Silver's ranch between us. What do you think about me owning a business here in town and living an hour and a half away? Do you think that's wise or would you recommend something else? I think I can make it work if I hire me some good help."

John grinned. Sometimes his intuition was surprising. His sweet Millie always said his intuition was better than any woman's. The idea that these two young bucks were beginning to think about their futures pleased him and fit right into his plans. That's what this town needed in order to grow and the more they grew, the better off it would be. Might even bring women to town without him having to send out letters. "I think that's a fine idea. With good help, it could work. But a livery is a full-time job, so I'm thinking it would have to be reliable help."

"That's the same thing I told him," Gil added. "He'll need help on the farm, too. Me and Sam know that we wouldn't be able to make it if it weren't for us being a team."

"That's a fact," Levi said. "I figure I can hire me some help to watch my livery in the evenings and overnight. I can maybe take a couple days off at my place and come to town and work at the livery. Hopefully any work people need doing can wait a few days if I'm at the farm."

"Worth a try."

"Sounds like you've got a plan. You'll put an offering on that land?" Big John knew the answer before he said it.

"Yes, I'm going to do it. It's going to take hard work and it's not going to be easy but one thing I have never done is run away from hard work."

Big John nodded. He didn't know a whole lot about Levi's past, but from the day he'd ridden into town a couple of years ago, the boy had been working hard. The old man who owned the livery had been in real bad health and he'd needed help. Levi had hired on and given it his all working for old Gus. Big John liked that about Levi, how he'd worked hard then made the man a solid offer to buy the livery. They'd finalized the deal and the payments were going to Gus's wife, who had gone back to be with family up north. Gus had told Big John he had been blessed by Levi's arrival.

Most people would have let the place continue on a downward spiral since Gus had not been able to keep it up, or they'd have let Gus die then bought the livery at a low price. Levi had taken that stable and made it look nice and given a good price for it. Now nobody was afraid to leave their horses overnight there.

"Are you thinking about getting a wife?" Big John asked, deciding to test the waters. Gil's eyes were bright Levi was more cautionary.

"I am," Gil said. "I tell you, watching Sam and Megan as they get their start out makes me think it'd be nice to have somebody else to talk to other than just my brother and Megan. She's real nice. I like her a lot but I don't know if I'm ready for a wife. There's a lot of tension going on between those two. They look like they're happy right now, though." He nodded toward his brother and Megan on the blanket. They seemed to be completely taken with each other. "I think they're gonna be all right. Though I have to tell you both before I came to town this week, I was kinda worried about it. Megan had been looking real sad in the evenings and I think my brother was even noticing that. Then she asked to come to town and despite our work, Sam agreed. When that happened I had my suspicions that things were turning for the better."

Big John agreed things were looking good. And just the fact that Gil had noticed all this made him feel much better about sending out a letter for him a wife. Then there was Levi and Matt and Deputy Donavan. They all needed a wife. He looked directly at Levi.

"What about you, Levi? You didn't answer my question."

Levi crossed his muscular arms. "I've been watching these mail-order brides coming into town and

I'm not sure what to think about it. I don't know if I could do that. I mean, it's worked out, it seems, but I can't imagine marrying someone I just met. But then again, there's nobody here to choose from, so I figure I'll work hard to build up my business and when the time is right and the woman for me comes along, I'll be ready." He hitched a shoulder up. "That will be better than now, and not being ready."

Big John took that in. "You don't think you have anything to offer a woman right now?"

"I know I don't and so I'm not offering anything. I've seen what a disaster that could be. I've grown up without anything. I've never said much about my life but my ma and me had to struggle…" He paused, looking as if he was lost in memories. Then he blinked and said with conviction, "No sir, I won't be looking for a wife until I'm ready and can give her everything she deserves. And I won't let some matchmaker make that decision for me."

Big John saw pain in the young man's eyes and he realized the young man carried some deep hurt inside his heart. Still, it was obvious he had his head on straight.

Big John liked his responsible attitude and he wondered what had happened to his daddy. Something *had* happened.

One thing Big John was certain of now, Levi would make a good husband.

CHAPTER ELEVEN

The social was fantastic. Megan loved Sam's quiet ways, his serious manner, but as he held her hand in the crook of his arm after they'd finished eating and they visited with friends, she felt at peace about her life. It was the first time in so very long…or maybe even the first time ever that she felt such peace.

And looking up at her husband, she knew it was because she was happy, and proud to be Sam McKay's wife. They would build a wonderful life together.

"Have a scone, Sam McKay." Ambrosia smiled broadly as they approached the table with the assortment of pies and desserts that everyone had brought to the social.

"You know I can't resist one of your cherry scones," he said, and she saw his kind smile soften his expression as he took the offered scone.

Chauncey ambled over, a grin on his grizzled face. "I'll take a couple of those too."

Mrs. Mulberry held the plate out to the miner. "Of course you will. I think you'd turn into one of my scones if it were possible."

He grinned then chomped down on one of the flaky desserts. "Ain't nothing like one of these." He turned his attention to Megan and Sam. "See you two have gotten yourselves figured out. You're lookin' mighty happy today. And after you saying that day before the stage arrived that you were going to meet that stage and send her packin'. That you didn't want no wife and no matchmakers were going to mess with your life."

The words cut through Megan's happiness as she realized this must have been his first reaction upon learning she was arriving on the stage the following day. Her gaze met his. "You were that against marrying a mail-order bride?"

"Chauncey, you should have remained quiet," Mrs. Mulberry scolded the miner.

"It's the truth. I come to town the next day just to see the fireworks. I was surprised when he instead took her down to the preacher's house and got hitched. It was a good change of mind, as I see it."

Megan had stiffened at the reminder that she'd come into Sam's life unbidden. "You were really that against me coming to town?"

"I had a strong reaction to realizing I was being set up. But then—"

"Set up? That would be how you would see it." Her skin felt warm again. All the beauty of the night before and the security that she'd begun to feel vanished in the truth. She had barged into his life and had married him with this marriage of convenience when in her heart of hearts she'd known he really didn't want to marry her. But she'd done it because she was afraid of her stepfather. It had been very selfish on her part.

"I don't see it that way any longer." His gaze bore into hers and his hand tightened on it when she tried to pull her hand from the crook of his arm.

Her insides trembled and again she felt vulnerable. It was of her own making, she realized. She had taken advantage of him because she had needed his protection. She tried to form a reply but her throat had clogged with tears and she battled, not letting them spill out for all to see.

"You ain't got nothing to worry about, little missy," Chauncey said, pausing between bites of his second scone. "I ain't never seen Sam look so happy."

"I haven't either," Mrs. Mulberry agreed. "Have you, Essie Jane?" she asked as her friend approached in time to hear the conversation.

"No, I haven't. Why, his smile has been firmly planted on his face today…well, not at the moment. What's wrong?"

"Everyone, I can speak for myself." Sam had begun to look as if a storm were brewing.

But she felt the same way. Her insides churned at the life they'd have from here on out—her thinking he hadn't truly been ready to settle down and maybe later, even if not right now, that he'd been trapped into marrying her. *Oh, how had she let this happen?* If she hadn't loved him, she wouldn't have felt so devastated by the thought. But now, she knew that to be fully satisfied in her love for him, she needed him to have come unconditionally into the marriage. And that could never happen now.

"I…I think this can be discussed later. I promised I would help Lucy and Gabby play games with the children. I better go help them." She pulled her hand from the crook of his arm, despite his hand still covering it. He let her go, maybe sensing that she needed some distance and that talking about this in front of their audience wasn't a good thing.

"I'll check on you soon," he said, not looking happy.

"Hope I didn't upset you," Chauncey said.

She didn't pause to say anything. What could she say? She was upset and there was no denying it. She needed some time alone to process it. Instead of heading to the area on the side of the church where the children's games were set up, she diverted and walked hurriedly down the other side of the church and then turned and walked behind a building where she found herself alone. She relaxed against the building and let her shoulders slump. Her world had just that morning held a hope she'd never experienced and now, it was gone, replaced by uncertainty on every level.

She closed her eyes and Sam's handsome, serious face appeared and her heart ached. *How was she going to ever come to terms with her life?*

"Hello, Megan," a familiar voice said as a hand slid over her mouth.

Her eyes flew open and she looked into the hard, angry eyes of her stepfather. Panic caused her stomach to drop to her feet. She struggled but his hand held her head roughly to the wood of the building and his other hand gripped her arm as if he would rip her arm from her body.

"Stop struggling and don't make a noise, or I'll shoot your man."

Shoot? Her gaze dropped to her stepfather's hips and there was a gun. She'd never known him to own a gun but sure enough, there it was. Her heart pounded now as she nodded, terrified and not sure what was about to happen. *How had he found her?*

What would he do to her?

~ ~ ~

Sam's heart pounded relentlessly as he listened to the flustered apologies of the ladies as he watched Megan walk away from him. He had to hold himself back from storming after her and telling her that she needed to ignore everything she just heard. Now was not the time. They needed to do this in private. He needed to let her know that there was no turning back for him, that he was glad that she had come into his life. He would make that completely apparent to her later, after she relaxed, helping the kids have a good time with Lucy and Gabby.

"Sorry about that," Chauncey said again. "You got a good lady there and I hate ta think I caused her to feel bad."

He looked at the miner. "You didn't mean

anything by it. But just so you know for future reference, I'm glad I married Megan and that she's in my life."

Chauncey grinned. "Well, I already knew that. That's what I said. It was just the pointing out that you didn't start out that way that I was sayin' earlier. I really hope I didn't hurt the little lady's feelings."

"Have another scone," Mrs. Mulberry said to the old miner. "I'm sure that Sam will be able to straighten it all out later. I know Megan cares for him. It was written in her eyes earlier." She smiled at Sam as she handed Chauncey another cherry scone.

Sam hoped she was right. He left them then, heading in the opposite direction of Megan, knowing if he let himself go near the playground, he'd go over there and interrupt her playing with the children and that wouldn't give her time to calm down.

Instead, he went to stand with a group of men including Trey, but his mind was on his bride.

"I thought Megan was going to help Lucy and Gabby," Trey said as Sam reached the group.

"She is. She headed over there a few minutes

ago."

"I just came from over there and she never showed up. We thought she might still be with you."

Puzzled, he looked around, scanning the area and trying to get a glimpse of Megan but not seeing her. Worry filled him. "I don't see her. I better go look around. She might have gone back to the hotel." This could be true but it wasn't like her; she had promised to be there for Lucy and Gabby.

"I'll come with you," Trey said, and fell into stride with him.

They circled by the side of the church to make sure Megan hadn't arrived after Trey had left but it just took one glance to see that she was not in the area.

"That's just not like her." Sam strode toward the front of the church and headed toward the sidewalk that would lead to the hotel. They were passing the livery when Gil stumbled out, holding his head. "Gil, what happened?" Sam caught his brother as his knees buckled.

"Megan…he took her." Gil managed to stay on his feet. "You've got to stop him. He took her on a horse."

"Who?" Trey asked before Sam got the question asked.

"Some man dressed in a fancy suit."

"Her stepfather." Sam's blood boiled and his fear for Megan ramped up.

"Someone get the doctor," Trey called.

Sam was worried for his brother but he was also worried for Megan. *What would her stepfather do? Was he going to hurt her?* He had to find her and he had to get to her fast. He shifted his brother to Trey. "I have to go find her. Take care of my brother."

"I'm coming with you," Trey said.

Gil yanked away from them and leaned against the wall. "I'm fine. Doc will be here. You go get my sister-in-law. Bring her home, Sam."

Sam shot a glance down the street at the crowd rushing toward them. Levi and Deputy Donavan were among those coming, along with Mrs. Mulberry and the doctor. He knew his brother would be in good hands. "I will." He gripped his brother's shoulder, squeezed hard then ran into the stables.

He went straight toward Gil's horse, glad his

brother had chosen to ride into town on the horse. Levi and Donavan ran into the livery as they were saddling up. They both grabbed horses after Trey told them what had happened. Moments later, following the way that Gil pointed, Sam rode out after Megan with the sheriff, Levi, and Deputy Donavan. It struck Sam hard as they followed the freshest tracks leading out of town that he didn't even know what Megan's stepfather's name was. He had never asked.

What was wrong with him? Had he not cared enough about her life to inquire about things that really mattered? She'd told him that her stepfather had had his own plan for her, but he hadn't in his own mind really thought that the man would come for her. The fact that he had made Sam believe he must be dealing with a half-crazed man or else a man so arrogant that things should be his way that he was dangerous. Sam was disgusted with himself.

He would get his wife back; he prayed she would be safe and then he'd tell her he loved her, cared for her and make clear to her that he had truly been blessed by whoever this matchmaker was. And he didn't plan on ever letting her forget it.

~ ~ ~

Megan hurt as she rode, thrown over the saddle; her ribs bounced up and down on a portion of the saddle horn. She could barely breathe, and her ribs hurt. "Let me up," she gasped once again, fighting to make the anger she felt known. The blood was pounding in her head as she watched the road behind them, wishing and hoping that she would see Sam riding to her rescue. She was worried about Gil, who had been in the livery looking at a beautiful horse when her stepfather forced her inside, his hand still firmly over her mouth. He'd obviously known who Gil was because he'd whispered that if she yelled or caused trouble, he would use his pistol. Her heart in her throat, she'd made no sound as he forced her into the livery. She'd watched Gil turn around and see her just before her stepfather hit him in the temple with the handle of his pistol. Only then had she gasped and fallen to her knees beside Gil, who was out cold.

Her stepfather grabbed her arm. "Get up. And if you scream, I'll shoot your husband when he comes to save you. Yes, I know you've married and that this kid is the brother. I have no trouble using my pistol."

She hadn't wanted anyone else to get hurt, so she'd kept her mouth shut as he'd gotten on the horse and then hauled her up and laid her over the horse in this ridiculous, awful position. Now she wasn't sure she would be able to move once she had her feet back on the ground.

"I'm not marrying your partner," she snapped. "I'm married."

"I'll have it annulled. Or when he comes looking for you, I'll make you a widow. This marriage has to happen or I may lose everything."

"What?" She couldn't believe it. "How does me marrying that horrible man save your business?"

"Because he likes you."

"Well, I don't like him." Everything was spinning as the blood rushed into her skull and that was when she glimpsed riders in the distance. They were riding hard. She blinked and tried to focus. Three of them…no, four, she realized as she focused better. And she focused on the horse in the center and her heart soared—she thought it looked like Sam's form. Her mind churned with thoughts about how she could get the pistol from her stepfather's hip. Her hands were tied, though, so it was hopeless.

~ ~ ~

Sam saw the horse and rider up ahead. He wanted to rip the man off the horse and drag him behind his horse for the way he had Megan hanging over the saddle horn like a sack of potatoes. She had to be hurting something terrible.

Trey motioned them to follow him as he headed toward a cut-through. "Follow me. Let's ride through the cut and stop them up ahead at the bridge."

Sam knew this was the smartest thing because if the man turned and saw them, there could be gunfire and Megan could be shot in the gunfight.

"I'm going to trail them while y'all ride ahead," Levi said, following them into the trees but pulling his stallion to a halt. "Just in case he makes a break for it and backtracks."

"Good idea," Sam said.

"Yes. Do that," Trey called, continuing his pace up ahead.

"Stay in the cover of the trees," Donavan told him as he and Sam rode to catch up with Trey.

Sam prayed for Megan and was glad that Levi would be watching from behind.

They rode hard and when they made it to the spot where the cut-through rejoined the road, Trey halted them. "They'll be here soon." He sent Donavan across the road into the trees on the other side.

Sam saw a place to position his horse closer to the curve in the road and moved his horse that way. He was getting in position when his instincts told him to climb onto the rock formation next to the road. He might have a better chance to distract Megan's kidnapper from above, so he tied his horse to a tree and then scrambled up the rocks as Trey took position up ahead. Moments later, he heard the horse approaching but it was Megan's voice that rang through the trees.

"You'll be sorry you did this. I'll never marry your business partner. I'll never get on a train with you. The minute you get me off this horse, I'll run and Sam is too smart to give you the opportunity to shoot him."

"Be quiet. What's gotten into you? You were quiet and knew your place back in St. Louis. Shut up."

"I'm not going to be quiet. And you're going to be sorry you came after me. You should have let me run away and gone on with your life."

Sam could see them, and the way Megan was slung over the horse and her captor had his pistol in his hand, resting on her back, ready to shoot anything that moved. Sam decided the safest way to take out her captor was for Sam to jump down and knock him from the horse and away from Megan. Trey or Donavan would go after the startled horse and save Megan. But this was the best way to get the man away from her and get her out of harm's way in case the man started shooting. Seconds later, they emerged from the trees and he knew this was his best chance. He dove.

The horse sensed him, and the stepfather yanked

his pistol up and got a shot off just as Sam slammed into him and they both tumbled to the ground.

~ ~ ~

The horse reared, as Megan heard the shot from the pistol and then her stepfather was knocked from the horse. As the horse bolted, Megan saw Sam slam to the ground, his body on top of the man she hoped to never see again. As the horse rushed forward, she saw blood on Sam's shirt. She screamed but could do nothing as the horse sped forward.

Suddenly, a horse raced along beside her and someone grabbed the reins. She was crying because she knew that the blood meant Sam had been shot.

"Sam," she cried as Donavan pulled her horse to a halt, jumped to the ground and gently lifted her from the horse's back.

"There, there, Megan," he said as he set her to the ground.

Her legs were asleep; her knees buckled beneath her and she folded to the ground.

Donavan knelt beside her. "Sheriff Trey is with him. Let me get you untied and then we'll go check on him. He's tough."

All she could think of was Sam. Bleeding—maybe dying on the ground behind her. "Hurry," she urged, her gaze riveted down the road where she could see Trey and another man. She thought it was Levi from the livery. They were kneeling by Sam. Donavan cut the ropes and helped her to her feet and she stumbled back to Sam.

"Sam," she cried, falling to her knees beside him. "Is he shot?" Her hands fluttered over his body, searching.

"He's unconscious," Levi said. "But he's not shot."

Thank the Lord. She cupped his face and kissed him. And suddenly his arms came around her and he was kissing her back. She started crying then, knowing this was her man and she was never going to let him go unless he sent her away.

"You're alive." She pulled back and looked into his serious eyes.

"If I'm not, then this must be heaven because kissing you can only be described as heavenly."

"Oh, Sam." She started to kiss him again then remembered Gil. "How is Gil? I was so worried about him."

"Doc was looking after him when we came this way." Trey stood up. "I'm afraid to say that isn't the case for this one. I'm sorry but looks like he hit his head when he fell."

Sam sat up and looked at the man who had been her stepfather for many years but all she could feel was relief. Sam pulled her against him, averting her face from seeing her stepfather's body. "You're safe now and that is all that matters." He stroked her hair and his lips against her ear sent warmth through her chilled body. "I thought I had lost you and it terrified me," he said. "I love you, Megan."

"And I love you."

He pulled back and looked at her. "I don't care what I said when I first learned there was a bride coming to town thinking I was her groom. I'll always be grateful you came into my life. Do you understand?"

She inhaled a shaky breath and nodded. "I'm so glad because I never want to leave you."

"That's perfect, since I never want to let you go." He cupped her face in his hands and his smile filled her with sunshine. "Let's go home and start our life together."

It was exactly what she wanted.

Coming soon, Elizabeth Chase's clean and wholesome novel, THE COWBOY'S MAIL ORDER BRIDE, book 4 in her exciting Mail-Order Brides of Sweet, Texas. You'll love this clean and wholesome mail order bride historical western romance series.

Books in the
Mail-Order Brides of Sweet, Texas

The Lawman's Mail Order Bride, Book 1

The Preacher's Mail Order Bride, Book 2

The Rancher's Mail Order Bride, Book 3

The Cowboy's Mail Order Bride, Book 4

About the Author

Elizabeth Chasen loves to write 'hopeful' romantic stories that inspire and entertain. All of her books are clean and wholesome Christian romance. She finds joy in bringing her fun characters to life and giving each of her couples their happy ending!

Always fascinated by Mail Order Bride historical romance, she enjoys creating her own stories to bring to her readers. Mail Order Brides of Sweet, Texas is the first of many series to come, so enjoy and she invites you to join her mailing list so you'll be the first to hear when her next exciting historical western romance is releasing.

Just go to: www.elizabethchasen.blogspot.com.

Happy reading!